Drew stood and reached for her as if he wanted to pull her into a hug

A part of Annie longed to accept the comfort he offered. But she couldn't. The stakes were too high.

Raising her hand, she said, "Don't. I just wanted you to understand."

"I had no idea." His voice was husky. "But you're wrong about one thing. I wouldn't have missed it. I could have taken compassionate leave to be there for both of you. You never gave me the chance."

Annie almost flinched at the loss in his voice. She couldn't continue to beat herself up wishing she'd done things differently. "So here we are, back where we started."

Dear Reader,

People often ask where I get the ideas for my
books. I wish the answer was clear-cut. The truth
is, my ideas come in bits and pieces from all sorts
of sources. And the process is different with each
book.

Welcome Home, Daddy started as the kernel of an
idea when a man from my community became
a military chaplain. Though I didn't know him,
I was struck by the sheer courage and dedication
of his decision. The sacrifices are huge, the hours
long, the work sometimes never-ending.

Then my questions began. What kind of man
chooses this challenge? What does it mean to his
life? And how in the world can he maintain a
romantic relationship, particularly if the love of his
life is opposed to his decision?

I played with these possibilities until Drew and
Annie were born. The magical part came when I
discovered they had a shared history and, surprise,
surprise, a son! I hope you enjoy Drew and
Annie's story—it's a special one.

I always enjoy hearing from readers at
carrieauthor@aol.com. And please feel free to stop
by my Web site, www.carrieweaver.com.

Yours in reading,

Carrie Weaver

WELCOME HOME, DADDY
Carrie Weaver

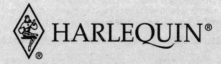

TORONTO • NEW YORK • LONDON
AMSTERDAM • PARIS • SYDNEY • HAMBURG
STOCKHOLM • ATHENS • TOKYO • MILAN • MADRID
PRAGUE • WARSAW • BUDAPEST • AUCKLAND

Recycling programs
for this product may
not exist in your area.

ISBN-13: 978-0-373-78323-6

WELCOME HOME, DADDY

www.eHarlequin.com

Printed in U.S.A.

ABOUT THE AUTHOR

With two teenage sons, three cats and a dog, Carrie Weaver leads a full life! She loves to wind down by indulging in chocolate and reading a good book—yes, the pages occasionally get smudged. The stories she writes reflect real life and real love, with all the ups, downs and emotion involved.

Books by Carrie Weaver

HARLEQUIN SUPERROMANCE

1173–THE ROAD TO ECHO POINT
1222–THE SECOND SISTER
1274–THE SECRET WIFE
1311–HOME FOR CHRISTMAS
1346–FOUR LITTLE PROBLEMS
1387–SECRETS IN TEXAS
1447–TEMPORARY NANNY
1476–BABY, I'M YOURS

In loving memory of my mom
Mary Ellen Tinker
1928–2009

ACKNOWLEDGMENT

I'd like to thank Marilee Hill for sharing her insights as a sign language interpreter.

Any errors made in translating the real world to fiction are strictly mine.

PROLOGUE

ANNIE TEETERED ACROSS the parking lot on Kat's ridiculously high stilettos. Take-me-now shoes, or so her friend claimed. Annie snorted. *She* certainly didn't want to be taken—now or ever again. That meant no hot, sweaty, ill-advised sex for her. When she ended her stint of celibacy—three years and counting—it would involve commitment, stability and a guy with a solid life plan. It did *not* include being dressed like a Goth hooker while embarking on a pity date, blind or otherwise.

Fighting the urge to readjust the red thong Kat had bought her for this special occasion, Annie eyed the expanse of asphalt parking lot looming between her and the side entrance to the lounge. The mid-May Arizona heat and synthetic fabric made her perspire in places she didn't want to think about.

Squaring her shoulders, she stumbled onward. She could do this. She'd endured worse than the Lycra miniskirt from hell.

Finally, Annie stepped inside the dimly lit lounge. After the harsh angle of the afternoon sun, she was effectively blinded, only able to discern vague shapes and shadows.

She detected movement as a human form separated itself from the bar and approached.

Blinking, Annie wished Kat had at least shown her a photo of the guy. He must be hideous. But then again, she recalled Kat saying he was drop-dead gorgeous, when she'd dated him through a popular online site. He simply hadn't rung her bells. Annie suspected it was because Kat's bells had already been rung by her almost-fiancé, Dillon, though they'd been on the outs at the time.

Or it might just mean this guy lacked the bad-boy charm that drew Kat like Silly Putty to shag carpeting.

Annie pushed her glasses into place, hoping it would help her focus. It didn't. Her transition lenses weren't transitioning quickly enough. She took them off and shoved them into her purse.

Ah, that was better. Things at a distance were still a blur, but at least she didn't feel as if she'd entered the Batcave. The Cantina Restaurant and Lounge was always kept appropriately dark and at subzero temperatures, she presumed to facilitate the impression of cool tropical breezes. Her nipples puckered at a particularly frigid gust.

She moved forward, almost walking past the looming figure.

"Grace?"

Then Annie remembered who she was for the evening. "Um, yes, that's me. Grace. You're Drew?"

"Yes."

She extended her hand at the same time he leaned in for a hug. He stopped and extended his hand at the same time she retracted hers and leaned stiffly from the waist.

Somehow, they managed to approximate an awkward hug.

Annie sighed. Kat would have handled this so much better.

"I'm glad you took pity on me and came out on such short notice," he said.

If only he knew. But it looked like the joke was on her. Because if anyone was on the pitying end, it would have to be this gorgeous specimen of man. Even in Kat's flashy clothes and sporting new blond highlights in her hair, there was no way Annie was anywhere near this guy's league. The realization made her glad she'd given up on the more macho specimens years ago.

"Um, no problem. Kat said you're shipping out in a couple of days?"

"Yeah. I'm at loose ends until I fly out day after tomorrow." He touched her elbow. "How about that table over there?"

Annie sighed in relief as she selected a chair. A table, not an intimate booth. She didn't know if she could handle being cooped up in an enclosed space with so much man. Not because he scared her—his warm brown eyes were surprisingly reassuring—but because he fairly oozed testosterone, from the top of his nearly shaved head, past his tanned, hard biceps, to his presumably sculpted abs. And she'd been avoiding such obvious masculine virility since she'd decided the course her life must take.

Sneaking one last, longing glance down his fine form, she suppressed a pang of irritation. If this guy hadn't attracted Kat, her friend had either been half-dead or really, really in love with Dillon the Deadbeat.

Annie licked her lips and searched for a topic of conversation "So, you're in the army?"

"Reserves. Got called up for a second tour of active duty."

"I'm sorry. That's got to be rough."

"It's hard on my mom. She worries."

"Yes, mothers have a way of doing that."

The waitress placed cocktail napkins on the table and glanced at Annie. "What can I get you?"

"Iced tea," Annie mumbled. A martini would have been so much more sophisticated, but she couldn't stand the things.

Drew ordered a beer.

The waitress rushed off, stopping to take several drink orders on her way to the bar. Poor thing, she seemed to be the only one on duty.

Annie glanced around the lounge. Finally, she asked, "Can you tell me about where you're going?"

He shook his head. "It's sensitive."

"That means dangerous?"

He hesitated.

Beneath the table, she crossed her fingers, hoping he'd tell her he was a supply clerk terrified at the sight of blood. And explain a detailed life plan that would do an underwriter proud. Because, despite her resolve, he was exactly the type of man who would have appealed to her pre-epiphany self.

Drew shrugged. "I'll be in a hot spot."

Kat probably would have said something witty, a double entendre about Mr. Hot Stuff.

But all Annie could do was swallow the lump in her throat and squeak, "How hot?"

He shifted uncomfortably in his seat. "So-so, I guess. I know I'll be seeing action and…this probably sounds weird, but…I've made sure my affairs are in order."

Translated, his chances of coming home whole and unharmed were slim. She'd heard of cases where soldiers had premonitions of being killed. Was that what he was trying to tell her?

"Like making sure your plants are watered while you're gone?"

"More like giving away most of my stuff and making sure my folks know where my important papers are."

Annie swallowed hard. Impressing Drew Vincent was a moot point. There would be no future for him. He was a marked man. And somehow, knowing that up front eased her mind, while at the same time making her very, very sad.

The waitress barely slowed as she deposited the drinks in front of them and was gone.

Annie sipped her drink while she tried not to think of this healthy, nice and totally together man being felled by an IED or suicide bomber.

Frowning, she tried to figure out what type of iced tea they'd used. Peach? No. And not raspberry.

He reached out and touched the back of her hand. "Hey, don't look so sad. I know how to take care of myself. I'll be fine."

Yeah, that's exactly what her dad had said only hours before plunging down the side of a mountain.

But she couldn't call this guy on his bravado. It might jinx him. Instead, she took a long drink, a little surprised at the way it warmed her throat.

Suddenly, it all became clear, her reason for being here. This wasn't about a silly blind date. It was about reassuring a guy who quite possibly wouldn't survive his tour overseas. It was about putting him at ease.

Annie twined her fingers through his and lied, "I know you'll be fine."

ANNIE WOKE UP WITH A start, aware that something wasn't right. It might have been the deep, even breathing coming from the other side of the bed. Or it might have been the muscular arm draped over her waist. But the dead giveaway was the now unfamiliar tenderness in her nether regions from a long night of hot sex.

Mostly it was her overwhelming urge to cry. Again.

Memories of sobbing all over Drew's im-

pressive shoulder after they'd made love
tempted her to pull the covers over her head.

She'd messed up big-time, after three years
of being so careful.

Drew shifted, removing his arm.

Annie held her breath.

Please don't let him wake up.

She had to get out of here.

Slowly, carefully, she slid out of bed. Gathering her clothes, she steeled herself not to
glance back at the bed. Forced herself not to
take one last, lingering look at the fabulous
man there. Because if she did, she might lose
it and dissolve into tears. Or worse yet, crawl
back between the covers and spend the remain-
der of the morning convincing herself that
Drew could be the kind of solid man of her
dreams.

The sheets rustled behind her.

Annie froze.

Carefully, she glanced around.

Moonlight spilled through the slats in the
wood blinds, softening the sharp planes of his
face. His eyes remained closed, but he muttered
something. Her chest ached at the thought that
a man so vital could be obliterated in a matter
of seconds.

She tried not to make a sound as she pulled on her clothes. Then she eased out the door and closed it softly.

DREW AWOKE AND immediately knew something was wrong.

He remembered he was in a hotel room. Still in Phoenix.

Then awareness assaulted him.

His gaze fell on the empty bed beside him. "Grace?"

He hoped her sweet voice would respond from the bathroom. But…nothing.

Closing his eyes, he fought a wave of disappointment. And something else, something much stronger.

He raised his head and groaned. "Shit."

Rubbing his temples, he willed the pounding to stop. He hadn't tied one on like that in years. It was a wonder he'd been any good to Grace at all.

But the memories came flashing back and he knew they'd been *very* good together.

Grace, alternately shy and passionate, hesitant and daring. He grew hard as he recalled her riding him, the long, slender column of her throat exposed to the moonlight as she threw her head back, her golden hair falling around her face, tousled.

Shit.

He also remembered her tears after they'd finished. And the tenderness he'd felt when he cradled her, whispering reassurances and words of love.

The endearments had simply been postnookie lies, hadn't they? Not really lies, because everyone fudged the truth with a one-night stand.

He wasn't sure. All he knew was that Grace had staved off that oppressive cloud of dread. The one that told him he might not make it through his tour.

CHAPTER ONE

More than two years later...

DREW STOOD OUTSIDE Grace's door, shifting from foot to foot. He wondered if the bouquet of mixed flowers was overkill.

He shrugged, then winced at the dull throb in his shoulder. A reminder of shrapnel that had mercifully missed all major organs, along with his body armor.

What if she was married and her husband answered the door? Drew would feel foolish, but at least he'd have a clear conscience. Thoughts of Grace had both sustained and haunted him in the Middle East.

Besides, Kat would have told him if Grace had someone in her life, wouldn't she?

Maybe that's why her voice had sounded a bit strangled when he'd called. He'd gotten the distinct impression she'd been surprised to hear from him. Even more surprised that he was asking for Grace's new phone number so long after their blind date. Kat had refused, offering instead to give a message to her friend.

When a week passed and he hadn't heard anything, he'd bought her contact information online for the low price of nine ninety-five. Ten bucks and a few minutes later, he'd found her. Annie Grace Marsh.

The door opened.

"You're early, Kat—"

"Grace." It was the only word he could choke out. The reality of seeing her in front of him— with new light brown hair and funky black-rimmed glasses—was overwhelming. The kid perched on her hip barely registered.

Her eyes widened.

And she slammed the door.

Of all the possible reactions, that was one he'd refused to consider. His top fantasy early in his tour had been of Grace throwing herself into his arms, inviting him inside for a repeat performance of their lovemaking. But now, the changes he wanted to make in his life dictated refusing. And having a fling with her again would pretty much negate his apology. Still, he was a man and couldn't help longing for the simpler days before he'd become uncomfortably aware of the finer distinctions between right and wrong.

He owed Grace an apology and he intended to follow through. He couldn't begin to contemplate making a career change until he had this settled.

He rang the doorbell again. Then he knocked. "Come on, Grace, open up. I just want to talk."

Except his motives weren't as pure as he wanted to believe. Maybe he wanted to see if they could somehow start over on a saner, slower note? See where it led? Something about Grace made it impossible to forget her. Something more than being good in the sack.

He knocked again, louder.

After minutes that seemed like hours, Drew knew when to admit defeat. But only temporarily. He would talk to her one way or another. He owed it to her, owed it to himself. And, probably most importantly, he owed it to the men and women he'd left behind in Iraq.

He dropped the flowers, turned and strode away.

AFTER THE KNOCKING STOPPED, Annie let the lullaby she was singing trail to an end. Opening her eyes, she gazed down at her son's beautiful face as she held him in the rocker while he drifted off to sleep. Tracing his velvety cheek with her finger, she marveled that she'd brought such a perfect child into this world.

Drew.

Her eyes misted when she thought of the night Micah had been conceived. It had been a mistake, an error in judgment she could never regret. Because she had been given a gift that made her embarrassment seem an insignificant price to pay.

But now she wondered.

Drew was *alive.* Her heart pounded.

Then the weight of what she'd done came crashing down hard.

ANNIE SMILED, WATCHING Kat push Micah on the swing. He laughed and kicked his chubby legs in no particular rhythm. "Higher," he squealed.

Annie bit her lip as she watched her friend comply. Logically, she knew the infant playground was designed for safety, but she couldn't quell her anxiety that something might happen to him.

She sighed with relief when Kat said, "Enough swinging for now, kiddo. I want to talk to your mom."

Micah protested as she took him from the swing, but Annie quickly distracted him with a plastic shovel and bucket. He happily plopped on his rear end in the sand to play.

Kat brushed her hair out of her eyes, her waist-length curls shining almost auburn in the sun. "Have you forgiven me yet?"

"It's not your fault. You didn't send Drew over to my place. You didn't give him my contact information."

"But I didn't tell you he'd called, either. You do believe I intended to, don't you? I'd never keep something like that from you."

Annie squeezed her friend's hand. "I know. I just wish I'd been…prepared. It was such a shock opening the door and seeing him there."

"Kind of like seeing a ghost? When I heard his voice on the phone…"

"It was worse than seeing a ghost." Annie's stomach started to churn. "I've done nothing but turn it over in my mind. How it'll affect Micah. How it might appear to Drew."

"Look, Annie, you did the best you could during a really tough time. The casualty list made it sound like he was as good as dead."

"I was so sick throughout the pregnancy. Then when they thought I might miscarry, I quit thinking about how Micah was conceived and just focused on delivering a healthy baby." That at least was part of the truth. The other part was so twisted, she didn't totally understand it herself. The bottom line was she'd convinced herself Drew was dead and that she didn't need to contact his family about the baby.

Annie gazed over the playground, trying not to think about that night with him. How equally wonderful and scary it had been to let go of her carefully constructed goals, if just for a few hours. To go back to being a little wacky, a little daring. It was the last time she'd felt free in a very long time.

"The truth is, I thought if I lost Micah it would be because I was being punished. Because I'd tossed away my rules for a night of meaningless sex."

"Was it meaningless?" Kat asked, her voice low. "I've never known you to have sex just for the sake of getting laid. Even during your wilder days."

Annie repressed a shiver. "He was the most beautiful man I'd ever seen and he had the kindest eyes. There was this…this electricity between us. Then it was over and I couldn't believe what I'd done. I cried."

"Aw, honey. You never said a word."

"Drew was so sweet that night…. So understanding."

"Then maybe it's a good thing he's back."

Annie shook her head. "Micah's mine. It's just the two of us. I've known since the first flutter of life that it would be him and me against the world. I decided then and there he wouldn't miss out on anything because he didn't have a father. I'd be his everything."

"And you have been. I totally admire how you've dedicated yourself to Micah. But maybe it's time to share some of the load."

"Micah is *not* a burden."

"You know that's not what I meant. All I'm saying is give the guy a chance. At the very least, he should be providing for his son."

Annie sipped her latte. She would have normally savored it. Just as she normally savored this Saturday-morning ritual with her friend.

"I don't want Drew's money." And then the truth slipped out before she could temper it. "I don't want things changing."

Warmth trickled over Annie's toes. She glanced down, suppressing a smile as she watched Micah pour sand on her foot. Reaching down, she steered his hand to the pail. "That goes in the bucket, sweetie."

He giggled and poured more sand over her toes.

Sighing, she decided shaking the grit off

her flip-flop was a small price to pay for Micah's delight.

"Think it through before you make a decision about Drew." Kat sipped her iced coffee. "Maybe go see an attorney first."

In Annie's shock at seeing Drew, she hadn't really considered the legal angle. "I wish he'd never come back."

"Yeah, who could've known he'd survive."

Annie's eyes widened. "I don't mean I wish he was dead. I just wish he…wasn't here."

"From what little I know of the guy, I'd guess he's not going anywhere."

And that was exactly what Annie feared.

THE DIAPER BAG BANGED against Annie's hip as she trudged across the parking lot after work on Monday.

"Mac. Cheese?" Micah smiled, excitement in his brown eyes.

"Let me guess. You want macaroni and cheese for dinner again?"

He nodded.

"You're going to turn into a big macaroni noodle." She tickled his ribs and his giggle warmed her heart.

"Me Mac."

"No, you're Micah, silly."

"Micah silly."

Kissing his cheek soundly, she was smiling as she rounded the corner to their apartment.

Her smile froze.

Drew pushed away from the wall, his muscular body blocking the walkway to her place. "Hi."

Annie felt her world tilt. She'd suspected this moment was coming. But she hadn't been able to figure out what she'd do.

"Drew."

"I need to talk to you."

He knew. And if he was in Phoenix to stay, he was going to demand joint custody.

Annie pushed her glasses up the bridge of her nose, stalling for time. "What's this about?"

He glanced around. The curtains in the apartment next door parted. "It's private. Can we go inside?"

It was on the tip of her tongue to refuse. After all, he was a stranger.

The irony made her want to smack her forehead. "I guess I know you're not danger-ous." She lowered her voice, "I mean, I *did* sleep with you."

"That's what I want to talk to you about."

Annie tightened her grip on Micah.

"Hey, no STDs here. You can sleep soundly

now. Well, I'm glad we had this little talk. See you later." She tried not to wince at her desperate attempt to deflect him.

"That's not what this is about. Besides, we used protection."

"Uh, yeah." Protection that had failed big-time. Was it possible he hadn't connected the dots?

She continued walking to her apartment, hoping against hope he'd simply turn and leave.

But he didn't. His hand at her elbow was light, but firm.

Reaching her door, she fumbled with the zipper on her purse and was finally able to locate her keys. Unlocking the door, she reluctantly gestured for him to follow. "Come on in."

Micah squirmed to be let down.

Annie fought the urge to hold him close and never let him go. She set him on the ground, and he ran through the wide arch to the family room, where he found his toy train set.

Drew stepped closer. He was still as physically imposing as she remembered. But his face was thinner, his eyes shadowed.

Annie swallowed hard. "I'm glad you came home okay." It was the truth. Even if it turned her world upside down.

"Me, too."

He reached out to touch her cheek, but

stopped. "I thought about you so often." His voice was husky.

"Really?"

"Yes. Did you ever think of me?"

Annie avoided his gaze. "I…was busy."

"Is there a man in your life, Grace?"

His use of her middle name irritated her. It reminded her of the harmless lie that had tangled itself into a big, hairy knot.

Licking her lips, she said, "No."

He stepped closer and brushed a strand of hair away from her face. His scent washed over her, reminding her of all that they'd shared in such a short, disjointed period.

"I owe you an apology."

Annie briefly closed her eyes. This could not be happening. She wondered if it were possible to die of guilt.

"I've relived that night we spent together," he continued, seeming not to notice her discomfort, "and can't believe I thought it was okay. I kind of exaggerated some stuff, made it sound like I wasn't coming back, so you'd feel sorry for me and, well, you know, go to bed with me. I figured it was no big deal, but it was. The way you cried…afterward. It's bothered me."

You lied to me? Then again, she was the last person to question motives.

She went into the family room, gesturing for Drew to follow. Snatching Micah's stuffed dragon off the floor on the pretense of tidying, she found herself holding it close, as if it could protect her.

"It was really sweet of you to apologize after all this time. Don't worry about it. I was overreacting."

He stepped closer and traced her cheek with his thumb. "No. Not overreacting. I treated you…dishonorably. And I want you to know how sorry I am."

"You didn't do anything wrong."

"Yes, I did. I was freaked out about going into active duty again and I reached out to you as a way to forget for a few hours. I shouldn't have…used you like that."

"I was a willing participant, remember?" Annie's cheeks warmed when she recalled exactly how willing she had been, and it had nothing to do with the Long Island Iced Tea the harried server might have given her by mistake. Even now, completely sober, she was drawn to him, wanting to feel his fingers in her hair, his warm breath on her neck. She could recall every exquisite detail of their night together, his scent, how he tasted.

She resisted the urge to glance at her son.

"No harm, no foul. You've apologized and it was nice of you, but unnecessary. Now, I'm sure you have somewhere you need to be."

She tried to edge him toward the door, but he didn't budge. Her maneuver simply put her uncomfortably close to a man who exuded pheremones.

"No, I need to say this. You were sweet and sexy and just about every guy's dream. But I could sense it wasn't something you would normally do. I should have been a better man and walked away."

She couldn't believe what she was hearing. Most men wouldn't have been bothered by shading the truth for sex. And coming back years later to apologize? Head injury perhaps? Or was it a ploy to check out Micah and look for a family resemblance?

"Your injury was severe?"

"How did you know I was wounded?" He flexed his shoulder out of habit, even though it hadn't troubled him in months.

She turned away. Her family room seemed entirely too small. All she wanted to do was scoop Micah up and flee.

As if sensing her thoughts, her son flung himself at her leg. "Mommy."

She brushed her fingers through his fine, silky, dark hair. His father's hair.

"Grace? How did you know I was injured?"

"It was on one of those antiwar Web sites that post information the mainstream media doesn't."

"Were you looking for me?"

"Yes," she said quietly.

"Mommy."

She glanced down at her son, who lifted his arms to her. Unable to resist, she picked him up and settled him on her hip.

"He's yours?" Drew asked.

Raising her chin, she said, "Yes, he's my son."

"He's beautiful."

"Yes, he is."

"How old is he, Grace?"

She squared her shoulders. She would do the right thing. Arguably, the honorable thing.

"First off, my name is Annie. Grace is my middle name. Micah is a little over a year and a half old. He was born eight months after you shipped out."

She waited for Drew to do the math.

She saw relief flash in his eyes.

"He was a month premature."

CHAPTER TWO

THE WORLD SEEMED TO shift as Drew absorbed Annie's statement. His emotions, the light, the very air in the room, seemed to whirl in a vortex of shock.

He concentrated on breathing for a moment. *In. Out. In. Out.* It was a technique his friend, mentor and camp chaplain, Orion Davis, had taught him when he'd first reached Iraq.

When he felt more in control, Drew waited a few more seconds to make sure he wouldn't go on the offensive. This was not the time to be confrontational.

The question uppermost in his mind could have been construed as a slur, but he had to ask it. "Is he mine?"

"Do you really need to—?" She waved her hand. "No. I forget that you don't know me, have no idea about my character. I was just a one-night stand to you."

Closing his eyes briefly, he wondered how he could have been such an ass.

"I had that coming. I royally screwed up. It doesn't mean I think any less of you."

"Don't you?"

He met her hard gaze. Her large, gray-blue eyes seemed almost exotic behind the nerd-girl glasses.

"No, I don't."

He read vulnerability in her eyes for a moment and then it was gone. "Micah is yours."

"Oh." He expelled the word as if someone had punched him in the gut. Which, essentially, she had.

"I don't expect anything from you. I really, truly, thought you were dead. Maybe I took the information from that Web site as gospel truth because it made things easier for me…to just forget that night we were together and focus on Micah. He needed me."

Her words stung him. "Was that night so bad?" *Was I so bad?*

She fiddled with the shoulder strap of the boy's overalls.

Her silence said it all.

"Never mind," he muttered, "don't answer that."

Running his hand through his hair, he tried

to think. He had a son. Probably. Maybe. What if he told his folks they had a grandson, only to find out later he'd been too trusting? They would be more than disappointed. That kind of letdown would be crushing, they wanted to be grandparents so badly. But they were in Michigan and didn't need to know until he was sure.

"I want a paternity test."

"You say you don't hold that night against me, yet you insist on a paternity test. I told you I don't want anything from you. There's no need for a test."

Drew allowed himself to glance at the large collection of photos arranged on one wall. Many were of Micah and an older woman who had Annie's smile. Family was obviously important to Annie. Surely she could understand his need to be a father to his own son. The need was as powerful as it was unexpected. But then again, finding out he was a father had been overwhelmingly unexpected.

"This isn't about money. This is about doing the right thing. If he's my son, he's my responsibility, and I want to be part of his life. And I will absolutely accept my financial obligations."

She snorted. "He's a child, not an obligation. I don't remember you being so pompous."

"And I don't remember you being so stubborn."

The child squirmed in her arms, his eyes wide. Drew tried to keep his cool.

"Grace—"

"My name is Annie. I'm sorry I didn't handle this better when Micah was born." She moved to the door and opened it wide. "But I'm going to have to ask you to leave."

"If he's mine, you can't just put me out of his life."

"I can certainly protect him from someone who doesn't seem to have his best interests at heart. Please go."

He'd tried to be calm, rational. And now he faced losing a son he'd never really had. Any thought of diplomacy went out the window.

"You'll be hearing from my lawyer."

Her voice was icy when she said, "Fine."

"Fine." He stalked out of her apartment. Even before the door closed behind him with a sharp click, he knew he'd royally screwed up again. It seemed to be his habit with this woman.

ANNIE STARED AT THE door long after Drew left.

She became aware of Micah's small hands patting her cheeks. He frowned.

"Sad?"

"Yes, I'm sad. But I'll be okay. Everything will be okay," she lied, wondering if anything would ever be right again.

DREW SPENT MOST OF the evening jogging at Tempo Town Lake, not far from his apartment building. His lungs burned with the effort. Inhaling deeply, he relished the smell of freshly mowed grass, enjoyed the sheer freedom of being able to run in public without being constantly on guard.

It made him all the more aware that the friends he'd served with and loved like family didn't have the same luxury. Some might not live to see home again. And those who did would be changed, just as he was. Time would tell if the changes in him would be a good thing.

Once he'd resumed civilian status, he realized he'd wanted to give back to his fellow soldiers. To make a difference.

But that was before Annie's revelation.

How could he begin to make this right? Certainly not by forgetting Micah existed, even though that was obviously what Annie hoped he'd do.

He'd never missed Orion more than at this moment. He needed his friend's down-to-earth counsel.

Drew pushed himself, running faster.

But he couldn't outrun his confusion.

He could almost hear Orion's familiar baritone.

Pray. Get on your knees and pray, buddy.

Drew picked up his pace, pushing himself to the limit. All the while talking to God in his head as if they were catching up over a beer. It was the only way he knew to pray.

I've got a son. What am I going to do?

Drew listed all his faults and the reasons why he couldn't be a father, as if God didn't already know the best and worst of him.

God was strangely silent on the subject.

Or maybe Drew simply wasn't listening hard enough.

He ducked under a low-hanging branch and kept on running.

Minutes later, he had his answer. The confusion lifted and so did his mood.

Guidance or endorphin rush? Either way, he was grateful for the result.

"I've…got to take…a chance."

He could piss and moan about the crummy timing, but it didn't change that he had an opportunity to be a father.

His feet pounded the asphalt as he tried on the new awareness for size. *A child. A gift. A life. A gift.* Drew had no idea why this awesome, scary, exciting event had occurred as the result of one crazy evening. But one thing was for sure. God had a plan.

ANNIE SAT AT THE SIDELINES on a bench and watched the high school football practice. She wouldn't be needed unless the coach motioned for her to come interpret for her student.

Despite longer days, a sore rear end and occasional bouts of sports-induced boredom, Annie wouldn't have traded these practices for all the desk jobs in the world.

Interpreting for a deaf teen at school was no less challenging than interpreting for a small child, it was simply different. Less hands-on, so to speak.

The coach instructed the team to run laps, which left Annie temporarily with nothing to do. Her mind wandered.

What was she going to do about Drew? Why did he pick now of all times to show up?

And he'd been understandably shocked. But his parting threat had been the stuff of her maternal nightmares. Though she supposed she may have never been ready.

Annie stood and stretched, admitting Drew hadn't asked for any of this.

The coach motioned her over and she joined

them on the field. Brett watched her closely as she signed the coach's instructions. Then it was back to the bench again.

And back to her problems.

Would Drew use her long hours against her if he fought for custody? The overtime provided by the football season was the only way she could prepare for surprise expenses. Otherwise, much as she enjoyed her job, she wouldn't be away from her son like this. She seemed to have little enough time with Micah these days as it was. Luckily, Kat had volunteered to take him during practice so Annie didn't have to pay for day care and feel guilty about him being away from home even longer.

She was jerked from her reverie by an extremely hard hit. She'd grown accustomed to the sound of pads colliding, an occasional grunt of pain. But this had been the sick thud of a body slamming the ground.

Anxiously scanning the field, she saw Coach jog over and kneel by the fallen player. She stood, hoping the boy was all right. Thank goodness Brett was a placekicker and didn't get much actual field time. It was hard not to mother the kid.

Coach helped the player up and he hobbled off the field.

She released a breath. The injuries never got easier. Maybe it was because she knew first-hand how quickly life could change.

On the field, Brett glanced in her direction, frowning.

Shaking off her worry about the injured player, she signed to him, reassuring him that everything was fine.

Still, she was grateful when Coach ended practice early.

The incident left her uneasy. On her drive home, rush-hour traffic gave her plenty of oppor-tunity to worry about Drew and what he might do.

She couldn't just ignore the problem and hope it went away.

And yet, she realized, that was exactly what she'd done since the night she'd spent in Drew's bed.

But the luxury of denial wasn't an option now. She would get Drew's number from Kat and call him tonight to set up a meeting.

When Annie let herself into the apartment a few minutes later, Micah's delighted squeal was music to her ears. She rounded the corner from the entryway into the family room. And froze.

Micah was sitting on the floor with his blocks. Drew sat next to him, smiling at his son.

His expression sobered when he glanced up and caught her eye.

Kat rose from the couch. "Look, Micah, your mama's home."

Her baby's smile was instant and gorgeous. A small replica of his father's.

"Hi, sweetie."

Micah ran to her, and she scooped him up in a hug.

After she kissed him soundly, she turned to Drew. "This is a surprise. But it's a good thing you're here. I was going to call you tonight."

Kat moved closer, her voice low and concerned as she said, "I left you a voice mail."

"I turn my phone off during practice so I'm not tempted to make calls when I'm bored."

"Practice?" Drew raised an eyebrow.

Annie went to set her purse on the coffee table near the couch, but thought better of it. Instead, she headed to the breakfast bar that separated the living area from the kitchen. It gave her the time she needed to collect her thoughts.

"Football. My student is on the team." She busied herself picking up scattered toys, while she balanced Micah on her hip. Drew probably thought her apartment seemed cluttered. She'd tried to brighten her hand-me-down furniture with colorful pillows and funky accessories, hoping to achieve the impression of eclectic decorating rather than single-mom-on-a-tight-budget.

"Here, let me help you." He stood, taking the toys from her and putting them in the toy box in the corner. "Your student? Are you a teacher? I thought you said you were a photographer."

Annie's face grew warm. "Um, I wasn't exactly truthful with you back then." Being a photographer had sounded more exotic. She'd figured a man like Drew would never be attracted to her very normal self, in her drab, monochromatic interpreting clothes.

"And yet you expect me to believe you about Micah now?"

Kat stepped in front of her. "It's my fault. I put her up to the date. I encouraged her to go outside her comfort zone and live a little. Her hair, her makeup, her clothes, all my dumb idea. The…half-truths were mine, too."

Annie gently nudged Kat out of the way.

"The lies were mine. I was an adult, I knew what I was doing. And I decided to play the game. As it turned out, the consequences were greater than I could ever have anticipated. I'm sorry, Drew."

He sighed. "I wish I could believe you."

Annie refused to glance away. "I wish you could, too."

CHAPTER THREE

ANNIE WAS BARELY AWARE of Kat slipping quietly out the apartment door. It was vitally important to make Drew understand. "Please listen to me. Let me explain?"

He flinched when she touched his arm. But he didn't turn away.

"I'm guilty of a lot of things. Hiding my head in the sand and believing what was most convenient at the time. I should have tried harder to find out what happened to you." She glanced at Micah, who seemed intent on removing his favorites from the toy box. Nodding to her… *their* son, she continued, "I thought I was doing my best for him. I was…wrong."

"What about before? I was almost a year into my tour in Iraq when I was wounded. Why didn't you contact me when you realized you were pregnant? That's what makes me question if I'm the father."

"Stop saying that."

"Believe me, it's not easy for me, either."

Taking a deep breath, she forced herself not to glance at Micah again. Instead, she recalled those frightening months after she'd discovered she was pregnant.

Somehow, she managed to speak. "I was ashamed and afraid, and wasn't able to face you. It took all my strength to get up every day. I was so sick I couldn't think of anything except keeping my health insurance and delivering a healthy baby."

"Couldn't or didn't want to?" Despite the accusation, his tone was soft, as if he'd begun to understand how difficult it had been for her.

"Maybe a little of both. I can't change what happened. But I will try to make it right if I can."

In the next instant, she was startled by a crash, followed almost immediately by Micah's cry.

She rushed toward where he lay crying by the breakfast bar, near an overturned stool. But Drew's long stride carried him there faster and he picked up her son and tried to cradle him.

Micah screeched and batted at him, his big brown eyes brimming with tears and pleading for his mother.

"Give him to me." She reached out and

Micah flung himself into her arms. "Where's it hurt, sweetie?"

He rubbed his chubby knee, his sobs subsiding.

"Thank goodness it wasn't his head." Gingerly, she touched the spot. "There's no bump. He must not have hit it hard."

Drew crowded her, reaching for Micah again. "Let me see. I have some first-aid training."

Micah clung even tighter.

She pivoted away from Drew. There was no way she would let go of her child when he was hurting and needed her.

"I'll keep a close eye on him. I think it's time for you to go—we can continue this discussion later."

Drew grasped her arm. "You just said you wanted to make things right, then you try to shut me out. I've missed the first year and a half of my son's life. His first words, his first step. I don't want to lose any more time with him."

Guilt and her promise warred with her maternal instinct. The result was simmering resentment.

"His first ear infection, his first temper tantrum." She ticked the items off on her fingers. "Oh, yeah, and you missed close to a thousand dirty diapers. But beyond that, you're forgetting one important detail. You were halfway around the world and would have missed those things, anyway. You were in no position to be a hands-on father."

He opened his mouth.

She held up a palm.

She kissed her son on both cheeks and wiped at his tears. "I think you're okay. Mommy'll get you a snack, all right?"

"Cookie."

She couldn't help but laugh. "Yes, you little manipulator, I'll get you a graham cracker."

"You can't stall and hope I'll go away," Drew interjected.

"I'm not stalling." She threw the words over her shoulder as she went to the small kitchen and returned with a graham cracker and a juice box. "I'm putting our son first."

Annie placed the snack on the coffee table and kissed Micah as she set him on the floor. When she was sure he was okay, she flicked the remote and brought up one of his favorite movies.

Then she turned and almost collided with Drew's very solid form. His close proximity only reignited her irritation.

She resisted the urge to poke him in the chest to get him to back off, but only because it might draw Micah's attention. But she didn't back down. "Before you tell me that you would have been here if you could, why don't you tell me why you never contacted *me*. Unplanned pregnancies happen all the time. Yet you didn't seem too eager to get in touch with me. I'll bet you just figured no news was good news. Let sleeping dogs lie and all that. If you even thought of me."

His guilty flush told her all she needed to know.

"Uh-huh. Just what I figured. So don't get sanctimonious with me. I was gathering the courage to call you when I ran a Google search for your name and found that Web site. And you know what? I *cried* for you. Because I thought you were a great guy and it hurt like hell to realize Micah would never know his father."

Annie ran out of breath.

Drew cleared his throat. "I don't know what to say."

"It seems you've said enough."

"I'm sorry. For what it's worth, I *did* think of you. Lots. But a pregnancy never crossed my mind. We used protection…."

"Obviously it failed. You said you wished you'd been there, but you have no idea what it was like. Maybe it would help if you understood a few things." She went over to the low bookcase that doubled as an end table and pulled out a large, leather-bound album. She nodded toward the easy chair that flanked the couch. "Have a seat."

Drew opened his mouth, but seemed to think better of protesting. He went to the sofa and sat. She got the impression he didn't much like taking orders in civilian life.

Tough.

She opened the photo album to the first page. "These are the ultrasound pictures. I was alone and scared and pretty much sick most of the time. I threw up after every single meal for three months. After that, it seemed like a reprieve that I only threw up in the evenings. For eight *months.*"

Tracing the blurred figure with his finger, he murmured, "This was Micah?"

"Yes. But it's the next page I really want you to see."

He flipped it over and stared at the photo for a long moment. When he looked at her, his eyes were bright with emotion. "He was so tiny."

"He was a month premature. He was sick and so alone in that nursery. I held him every chance I got, terrified it might be the last time. So when you talk about the things you've missed, be aware that some of it was pure hell."

Drew stood and reached for her as if he wanted to pull her into a hug.

A part of her longed to accept the comfort he offered. But she couldn't. The stakes were too high. She'd lost her head with Drew once and didn't intend for it to happen again.

Raising her hand, she said, "Don't. I just wanted you to understand."

"I had no idea." His voice was husky. "But you're wrong about one thing. I wouldn't have missed it. I could have taken compassionate leave to be there for both of you. You never gave me the chance."

Annie flinched at the note of pain in his voice. But she couldn't continue to beat herself up, wishing she'd done things differently. "So here we are, back where we started. This isn't getting us anywhere. Micah's hungry, I'm tired."

"I'll go. For now. I'm in the reserves and don't know what the future holds. If we can't come to some sort of understanding soon, I'll have no choice but to talk to an attorney."

Once again, his threat hung in the air long after he'd let himself out of her apartment.

DREW SAT IN HIS truck, the engine idling as he decided whether stopping in at the Davises' house was such a good idea.

He thumbed through the photos in his cell phone until he came to the one that made him catch his breath every time he looked at it.

It was taken at Orion and Beth's anniversary dinner when both men went home on leave. Orion had joked that it made them look like the Huxtables from *The Cosby Show*. All Drew saw was a couple who had loved each other through the ups and downs of a long marriage and still actually liked each other.

Drew missed his mentor every day, but today especially. The big, gentle bear of a man had time after time shown the amazing ability to laser through the B.S. to the core of any problem. And Drew desperately needed that clarity now.

So he sat parked on the street outside Orion's house, where his widow, Beth, lived with their teenage son. Their two adult daughters always seemed to be dropping by, and Beth babysat her granddaughter, Libby, after school each afternoon. It made for a busy, sometimes boisterous household.

It had only been two weeks since Drew's last visit, but already it seemed a lifetime ago. Especially since he couldn't give Beth an answer yet to her question. But if he couldn't talk to Orion, talking to Beth was the next best thing.

Taking a deep breath, he shut off the engine and got out of the truck. He made his way up the walk past the blooming bougainvillea.

The smallest occupant, Libby, opened the door wide.

"Hey, munchkin. Is your grandma home?"

"You bring more presents?"

"Not today. Soon. Would you get your grandma?"

"Sure." The door shut as Libby went to find Beth. At least that's what he hoped she was doing.

He couldn't help but grin. She was a cute kid, with chubby cheeks and sparkling brown eyes.

The door opened again a few minutes later and Beth's welcome soothed him.

"Hello, Drew, what a wonderful surprise. Come in. I was helping Damian with his homework."

"I didn't mean to interrupt—"

"Heavens, no. You saved me. It's algebra and I'm not much help at all."

He followed her to the large, homey family room, with the foosball table in the corner and two overstuffed brown love seats.

"Would you like a soft drink or iced tea?" Beth asked over her shoulder.

"No, thank you. I just came to talk, if you have a few minutes."

"I'm always available to talk." She laughed as Libby scampered into the room, filched a cookie from the jar on the counter and left just as quickly. "Well, almost always."

They sat on the couch and Beth waited, but Drew wasn't able to get any words out. Would she think less of him when he told her about Micah?

"I take it you've been thinking about your future?" she prodded gently.

"Yeah." That was an understatement. He'd spent more than one sleepless night wondering if Orion's faith in him had been misplaced. And that was before learning about Micah had thrown him for a loop.

"Did you come to a decision?"

His life had taken a sharp detour since he'd last talked to Beth. He couldn't just blurt out that he had a son. Or the details of how Micah had been conceived.

"I'm still not sure. How do I know if this chaplain thing is right? I mean, *really* know? It's not like there's been a lightning bolt or even a gut feeling."

Her laugh was musical. "I bet your gut is churning. You're not sure you're up to the task. You think almost anybody would be better than you."

He released a breath. "How'd you know?"

"That's how Orion felt before he took the plunge. Then seminary convinced him he'd *never* cut it. He only changed his mind later."

"I can't imagine him being unsure of himself. He was the best."

"Yes, he was." She glanced away.

"I'm sorry. I don't mean to make things harder for you. I shouldn't have come—"

She grasped his arm. "No. Thank you. I like being reminded. I feel closer to him."

"How can you be so kind when you've lost so much?"

"Because I've been given so much."

Drew didn't know what to say. Her quiet faith humbled him. Her goodness and gratitude made him feel guilty.

"Drew?"

"Yes?"

"Orion was an excellent judge of character. He could size up a soldier in a way that I swear saw right down to the man's soul. He told me you had what it took. Are you going to call him a liar?"

"No, ma'am."

"Then do me a favor. Where do you keep photos of your tour?"

"I've got them in a digital file on my laptop."

"Print out a few. Place them where you can see them every day. Make it a point to look at the faces first thing when you get up in the morning and before you go to bed at night. I suspect you'll soon have your answer."

Drew squeezed his eyes shut. "You don't fight fair."

"No, I don't."

He opened his eyes. "I'll do it for you."

"No, you'll do it for yourself. And for the people who need you."

"Yes, ma'am."

He waited for her to fill the silence, but she didn't. In her own way, she was as good a counselor as her husband had been.

"Beth?"

"Yes?"

"I found out I have a son."

She studied him for a moment. "This is happy news?"

"Yes, I think so."

"Then congratulations." She hugged him, her clean scent washing over him. "You'll make a wonderful father."

"I hope so. But it changes everything."

"Are you sure?"

The past couple of days, he'd incessantly turned it over in his mind and come to the conclusion that he believed Annie. It was a gut instinct based on what little he knew of her.

She didn't seem to hesitate to take responsibility for her mistakes. And he couldn't see her trying to palm off her son on him if it wasn't true. Besides, he had been the one to initiate contact.

"I'm pretty sure he's mine. I've asked for a paternity test, though."

Beth chuckled. "No, I mean are you sure that it changes anything?"

"Of course it does. I've already missed almost the first two years of Micah's life. There's nothing I can do to get that time back. I can only make sure I'm here for him now."

"You've a difficult choice to make. It's never easy when children are involved."

"Did Orion…ever regret it? Missing so much of his kids' lives?"

"Yes…many times."

"But he did it anyway."

"Yes."

"I'm not half the man he was." He hadn't dared voice his greatest doubt before.

"You can be, Drew. Follow your heart. Look at those pictures. Pray."

That's exactly what he'd been afraid she would suggest.

CHAPTER FOUR

ANNIE STARTED THE DVD in the hope that she and Kat could have twenty minutes of semi-uninterrupted time to talk. With an energetic toddler around, it was highly unlikely.

She held her breath as she waited for Bob the Builder to work his magic.

Sure enough, Micah scooted closer to the screen.

"I owe my last scrap of sanity to Bob," she commented.

Kat handed her a bottled beer. "To Bob. At least he's better than The Wiggles."

"You've got that right. To best friends." She clinked her bottle against Kat's.

"Best friends," Kat echoed. "How long till the pizza gets here? I'm starving."

Gesturing for Kat to follow, she went to the breakfast bar and sat on a stool. "You're always starving. It's not fair that you can eat anything and not gain an ounce."

"I'm blessed with a fast metabolism. You've got curves I would kill for."

"The remaining five pounds of baby weight."

"All in your boobs. Not fair."

"So get pregnant."

Kat sighed. "Dillon isn't ready. He wants me all to himself."

Annie made a noncommittal noise. Dillon had Peter Pan written all over him. But a friend didn't point out glaring faults in someone's fiancé.

"Besides, I have so much fun with Micah, then I can give him back when you get home. It's a win-win."

"I owe you big time, Kat."

"You'd do the same for me."

"Absolutely." Annie figured she'd pretty much lay down her life for Kat. Well, she would've before Micah, that is. Now that she had him to consider, she'd simply stop a speeding bullet with her teeth. Motherhood necessitated heroics.

The doorbell rang and Annie paid the delivery guy, returning to the family room with the pizza.

"Pizza!" Micah squealed, clapping his chubby hands as she placed it on the coffee table.

"Second only to macaroni and cheese."

"Me, Mac."

Kat chuckled. "Don't even go there. It's like a bad session of 'Who's on First?'"

"You learn quickly."

"When I have to."

Annie pulled an old blanket from the coat closet and spread it on the floor in front of the TV as Kat cut up a slice of pizza for Micah. "There you go, sweetie," Kat said. "Try to keep it on the plate."

Micah giggled.

"I don't know if it's the movie that made him laugh," Annie said, "or the absurd idea that he keep the food on his plate."

"Knowing him, it's a coin toss. The kid loves to make a mess."

"Help yourself while I get his juice."

"I already did."

Annie raised an eyebrow at Kat's huge slice as she returned with Micah's favorite sippy cup.

Taking a smaller piece herself, she settled back against the couch, paper plate balanced on her lap.

Kat's tone was nonchalant when she asked around a mouthful, "Details, woman. You said Drew mentioned an attorney?"

Annie swallowed hard. The pizza dough was suddenly tough to get down. "Yes. But I called Drew last night and convinced him to give

Micah a little time to get used to him. He's, um, going to meet us at the park tomorrow after work. Just a quick, casual visit. I was afraid he might want to take Micah overnight or something, and I don't think I could handle that. It's going to be a huge adjustment."

"Yeah. Micah seems to like him, but…"

"What do we really know about him? I need to find out what kind of person he is. Do you remember any important details you learned when you dated him? Did anything strike you as…odd?"

Kat tangled a hand through her long curls, flipping her hair behind her shoulder. "Seeing him again, I think it's odd I didn't appreciate how incredibly hot he was."

"Be serious. This is important."

Sighing, Kat said, "Okay. We only went out twice. I remember he was polite, great sense of humor, nice-looking. The buns of steel thing was definitely an attention getter."

"You claimed you didn't notice." Annie eyed her friend suspiciously. "Are you sure you didn't sleep with him?"

"I'm kidding. Geez, you're usually not this literal."

"You said you'd be serious. Anything about his character that might be…suspect?"

Kat crossed her arms over her chest. "Yeah, he was a gentleman. Not even Dillon was that…thoughtful. And I *loved* him."

Annie wondered if her use of the past tense was meaningful. Was Kat having second thoughts about Dillon? Annie prayed her friend came to her senses and dumped the guy before she got hurt too badly.

But Annie knew better than to voice her opinion. She'd learned that lesson her senior year when Kat had been dating Manny Porter. Her friend hadn't spoken to her for weeks after Annie expressed concern. Until Manny was caught under the bleachers with a cheer-leader, to the dismay of Kat and her Chess Club crowd.

Besides, Annie was on a mission. "So I guess Drew never let anything slip about his medical history or credit rating, huh?"

"Nope." Her face brightened. "No mention of an arrest record, either."

"Oh, that's comforting."

"Great. I shouldn't have said anything. I forgot you worry about every little thing now that you're a mother."

Micah stood and squealed, dancing in time with the show's theme song, pizza in his hand.

Annie smiled at his enthusiasm. Sometimes

her love for the child took her by surprise. She hadn't known it was possible to love another human being as much as she did her son.

Nodding toward Micah, she said, "Someday you'll understand." Annie picked up a throw pillow and fingered the fringe.

"I suppose." Kat flipped open the pizza box and selected another slice.

Annie was too busy worrying to eat much. "I wonder if I can find out online if he has a record. I mean, he *seems* normal. What if he's trying to lull me into a false sense of security?"

Kat patted her hand. "Hey, I'm a pretty good judge of character. I wouldn't have set you up if I thought he was an ax murderer."

"I could do without your reassurances. Your choices in men are sometimes lousy."

"I'd be offended if I thought I had a leg to stand on. I've picked a few winners over the years."

Annie made a noncommittal noise.

Kat snatched the throw pillow and smacked her lightly upside the head. "Then do a background check on him. For twenty bucks online you can find out almost anything."

"It's tempting. I would hate to invade his privacy like that…. But Micah's safety has to be my first priority."

"Exactly. If nothing else, you can check the

county court records for free. Find out if he's been married and divorced six times or has a felony conviction. And you could do an Internet search on him."

"I suppose."

"We'll do it together after the squirt goes to bed. We can be like Nancy Drew."

"There's only one of her," Annie pointed out.

"Scooby and Shaggy?"

"I think not."

"Okay, Velma and Daphne?"

"Only if you're Velma and I'm Daphne."

Kat shook her head. "No way. Just because I'm an accountant doesn't mean I have to be the nerd queen."

"Once a nerd queen, always a nerd queen. I bow to your great prowess in the chess club."

"You're never gonna let me live that down, are you?"

Annie bumped her with her shoulder. "Nope. Never. Funny how life turns out and our roles are reversed. Now you're the outgoing one and I'm sidelined from the dance."

"Only because you've chosen to sideline yourself."

"I'm a single mom."

"Who are you kidding? You sidelined yourself way before that. What I want to know is if you're ever going to tell me what happened to cause all this caution? I trace it back to that year I traveled so much for my job."

Annie avoided her gaze. "It was more of a slow evolution as I gained knowledge and maturity," she lied. For some reason, she'd never been able to confide in even her best friend about the catalyst. Maybe because Kat would have handled the episode much differently.

"Uh-huh."

"Anyway, I need to be mature, responsible and stable for Micah."

Kat's smile faded. "Yeah, I can't argue with that. Anybody could tell he means the world to you. Let's just hope Drew understands."

Her words stayed with Annie long after their fruitless Internet search for any deep, dark secrets the man might have hidden away.

She was reluctant to let Drew disturb the cozy world she'd built around Micah. They were safe; their future looked bright. And Drew was a big, fat unknown.

In Annie's experience, unknowns were rarely a good thing.

DREW WHISTLED AS HE set his car alarm and headed up the walkway toward the playground.

He stopped a few feet away from the designated play area, watching Annie scooting slowly down the slide with Micah on her lap. Speed obviously wasn't the objective. Micah's smile was wide, though, so Drew figured the kid was enjoying himself.

The sand crunched beneath his running shoes as he walked over to meet them at the bottom. "Hey."

Annie shielded her eyes from the late-afternoon sun with her hand, glancing up at him. "Hey, thanks for meeting us. For some reason, there doesn't seem to be another kid in sight and we could use the diversion."

She stood, balancing Micah on her hip. He struggled to get down, but she held him tightly. Her voice was overly bright when she said, "Micah, Drew's here to play with us."

Drew raised an eyebrow and grinned, trying unsuccessfully to avoid imagining the ways he could play with her.

She must have followed his train of thought because her cheeks grew pink. "I mean, he's here to play with you," Annie amended.

Not for the first time, he felt a stab of nostalgia, a wistfulness that his days of casual sex were in the past.

"Yeah, kid." He tousled the boy's hair. It was silky to the touch. "What do you want to do?"

"Swing!"

"Okay." They made their way to the swing set, where Annie wedged Micah into a baby seat that seemed too small for the toddler.

Shrugging, Drew decided not to make a big deal out of it.

"Push," Micah commanded.

"Yes, sir." Chuckling, Drew positioned himself behind the swing and pushed gently. The sun was warm on his face and a slight breeze kept the temperature pleasant.

"Higher."

"That's high enough," Annie warned.

"Your mom says this is high enough."

Micah kicked his feet in a futile effort to propel the swing himself.

"Let's start off slow, big guy."

In more ways than one. Although Drew wanted to jump in and make up for all the milestones he'd missed. As if he could cram almost two years' worth of experiences into one short afternoon.

"Thank you for understanding," Annie said softly beside him.

If it hadn't felt like she was hovering, he might have enjoyed her presence. Or if he was under the impression she wanted to spend time with him. But he had no such illusions.

He noticed the sheen of perspiration on her upper lip. "You can go sit in the shade if you'd like. It's turning out to be a warm day."

She hesitated.

"We'll be fine. You'll still be close."

Annie seemed to gauge the distance between the bench and the swing. Finally, she nodded and trudged the few yards away. Letting go seemed difficult for her.

Drew shook his head, reminding himself that he'd only been a father for a week. She'd been a mother for almost two years.

The boy chattered about everything and anything as Drew continued to push him: the sky, a mockingbird in the nearby eucalyptus tree, an airplane. Airplanes seemed to capture his attention the longest. He watched one until it was a tiny speck in the distance.

"You like planes?"

The boy held his arms out at his sides as if he were flying.

Laughing, Drew marveled at the kid's joy.

"You gonna be a pilot? Should I start saving for the academy?"

"Most certainly not."

He thought Annie was joking until he glanced over his shoulder and saw her tight expression. She was ticked off at him.

"Well, the army *is* superior. Maybe he'll take after his dad and stay on the ground."

"Don't go putting those ideas in his head. He's just a baby. Besides, he already knows a few of his numbers, so I figure he's going to be an accountant like his aunt Kat."

"That's a stretch at his age."

"No more so than your army propaganda."

He chuckled. "Don't tell me you're a pacifist?"

"My political views are none of your business. Just stick to the safe topics with Micah, okay?"

"And those are?"

Her expression relaxed and she actually smiled. "Potty training is at the top of the list. If you can convince him to wear big-boy pants and go in the potty, I'll love you forever."

"Hmm. That's all it would take?"

"You have no idea. Most boys don't potty train till they're around three. And this child is already showing signs of being more stubborn than most."

"He must get the stubbornness from you, then, because I'm very flexible."

"Humph."

Micah kicked his feet. "Higher!" he screeched.

Drew stepped in front of the swing. "Is this baby contraption too small for you, big guy? Hey, I've got an idea."

He lifted Micah out and moved to a regular swing, where he sat down, plopping Micah on his lap.

The boy grasped the chains and looked expectantly over his shoulder at Drew.

"I don't think that's a good idea," Annie called.

He was so intent on sharing the moment with Micah, he barely heard her. Pushing off, he stretched out his legs.

Micah's responding giggle was all the encouragement he needed. With one arm wrapped securely around the boy and the other hand gripping the chain, he pushed even higher. The breeze felt wonderful on his face. He almost felt free. Freer than he'd felt in years.

Micah held out his arms. "Flying."

"We *are* flying. Feels good, huh?"

They picked up speed, the trees blurring as they arced higher.

"More!" Micah shouted.

"Your wish is my command."

"No!" Annie's scream finally caught his attention.

Over his shoulder he was perplexed to see her racing toward them.

She dodged around to the front of the swing.

"Stop!" She held out her hand like a traffic cop.

Micah protested as Drew dragged his feet in the

sand to slow them down. When he realized how pale Annie was, he stopped them completely.

"What's the matter?"

"Are you trying to kill him?" Annie wrenched Micah from Drew's grasp. The toddler wiggled, but couldn't break her hold.

"He's okay, Annie. Nothing happened."

"No thanks to you."

He noticed her wet face. "You're crying."

"Damn right I'm crying. I trusted you to take care of him. I should have known better."

"We were just having a little fun. He was safe, I had a good grip on him."

"Just having a little fun." Her eyes blazed. Annie seemed to have instantly switched from panic to lioness protecting her cub. "Do you know how easily he could have fallen and broken his neck? You could have killed him. I will *not* allow you to endanger my son. Until you can prove to me that you take the responsibility seriously, don't even ask for unsupervised time."

Drew shook his head. "You're blowing things out of proportion."

"Micah's safety is my top priority. I know what's safe and what isn't. You definitely are *not*."

CHAPTER FIVE

FIFTEEN MINUTES AFTER sinking to the park bench, Annie's knees had stopped shaking, but she still felt trembly inside.

"Down," Micah said, pushing against her chest with his hands.

She forced herself to loosen her grip and set him on his feet.

That made him happy for a few short minutes. Then he was back again, whining, and it took every ounce of willpower she had not to scoop him up once more.

But Drew obviously thought overstimulating him was a good idea. It would serve him right to see the consequences of his actions.

"Swing," Micah demanded.

"Sorry, buddy, your mom says no." Drew handed him a shovel. "Here, let's dig in the sand."

"Swing."

Annie folded her arms. "It's not fair to make me the bad guy."

"But you *are* the bad guy."

"I'm the voice of reason. Someone has to be mature here and you're obviously not the one."

"I happen to be a responsible guy. What's this really about, Annie?"

"Why does it have to be something to do with me? Why can't you admit you were wrong?"

"Because I didn't do anything wrong."

She ignored that, knowing her response at the moment would be "Did, too," which would shoot down her argument for being the mature one. So she opted for silence, grateful when two mothers with several children in tow converged on the playground, saving her from responding.

Micah eyed the children for a moment, then returned to playing with Drew.

As for Annie, she watched his patience with Micah and refused to be swayed. He took a second shovel and helped Micah fill the bucket. Something about seeing his strong, tanned hand cradle the plastic implement made her get all misty.

Wasn't this what she'd always wanted for her son? A strong, intelligent guy to bond with?

Shaking her head at the unwanted thought, she pretended to watch the other children play, while keeping track of Micah out of the corner of her eye.

Once he was engrossed in building his version of a sand castle, Drew stood and brushed the sand off his jeans. He walked to the bench and sat down. "Hey, I understand you've been his only parent up till now, and it's hard to let someone else step in. But you've got to work with me here."

"I *am* working with you. But I can't stand by and watch you endanger my son."

He grasped her hand. "You don't trust me much, do you?"

"I don't even *know* you. And all of a sudden I'm supposed to turn over the most important person in my life. He's just a baby. He might not even be able to tell me if you did something… wrong."

Drew released her hand. "I'm no child molester."

Annie ignored a twinge of guilt. Keeping Micah safe was more important than tiptoeing around Drew's feelings.

"How can I be sure?"

"By getting to know me." He sighed. "I understand your protectiveness. Being a parent is scary for me, too. I want to do things right and I guess there's a learning curve."

His admission touched her. It was hard to believe such a big guy could be afraid of a small boy. But she remembered her first few days caring for Micah.

"You should have seen me the first night I had him all by myself. My mom had gone home to Payson. I panicked because I was sure I wasn't ready. But Micah needed me. And you know what? I didn't do things perfectly. I did some dumb stuff. But it still worked out okay because I loved him and wanted what was best for him. Before I knew it, he was six months old and the healthiest, happiest baby around. I'd somehow managed, mistakes and all."

"Are you going to allow me to make mistakes?"

She hesitated. "I can't say I won't freak out if I see danger. But I'll try to cut you some slack. I didn't stop to think how hard it must be for you, having all this thrown at you. It's not like you had eight months to get accustomed to the idea like I did."

He draped his arm behind her, over the wooden back of the park bench, his red Cardinals T-shirt stretched across his broad chest. "All I ask is for a chance. Because I really want this, Annie. I really want to be the best possible dad for Micah."

"Just be more cautious. Babies' heads account for more of their body weight proportionally than an adult's. They fall headfirst. A tumble from any height could be disastrous."

Understanding glimmered in his eyes. He nodded. "I promise I'll be more careful about heights."

Annie released a breath. "Good."

"Maybe we can do something together on Saturday, the three of us? It'll give you a chance to fill me in on the dos and don'ts where Micah's concerned."

"This Saturday?" Annie stalled for a moment. Supervising his time with their son was a good thing. And so was bringing him up to speed on how to keep Micah safe. But she hadn't really anticipated what it would mean to have him in their lives on a regular basis. Of course he would want to see his son more than just on holidays.

"Yeah. It'll give all of us a chance to adjust to me being in the picture."

"I have to work the football game."

"During the afternoon? I thought high schools had their games at night."

"They do. But I need to be there by five."

"I'll have you back in plenty of time."

Annie racked her mind for any other plausible excuse and couldn't find one. "In that case, okay."

What really disturbed her was the small spark of anticipation she felt. This was all about Micah, wasn't it?

WHEN DREW ARRIVED at Annie's apartment Saturday morning, he was surprised to see a bunch of toys and baby items outside her door.

He eyed the pile as he rang the bell.

Annie opened the door, fresh-faced, her hair drawn back in a ponytail. She looked all of about sixteen. "Come on in. I'm changing Micah one more time before we leave."

Micah dashed out of his room, completely naked.

He waved, giggled and ran back to his room.

Annie sighed. "We'll be just a minute. There are days I can't seem to keep clothes on that child."

"He's a free spirit, huh?"

"Apparently. My mom says I was the same way when I was his age. But back in those days, it was okay for kids to run around in only a diaper, weather permitting."

Drew chuckled. "So you weren't always this…careful."

"Apparently not."

"Anything I can help with?"

"No. More attention will only encourage him. He thinks it's a game." She scooped up Micah as he dashed out of his room. "No, you don't, mister. We need to get some clothes on you if you want to go on a picnic."

"Picnic." Micah clapped his hands.

"He's excited. He was up extra early this morning," she said over her shoulder.

"What time is extra early for him?"

"Five-thirty. Usually he doesn't wake up till about six. Six-fifteen if I'm really lucky."

"Wow, that shoots the heck out of sleeping in on the weekend."

Annie placed Micah on the changing table along the wall by the door and swiftly diapered him. Then she started wrestling him into his clothes, a maneuver that resembled dressing a greased pig.

"I gave up on sleeping in a long time ago. I'm just grateful he sleeps through the night and usually allows me close to eight hours. He had colic when he was an infant, and it was pretty rough."

Drew wandered around the room, taking in the Winnie-the-Pooh theme, the large mural of Pooh, Rabbit and Eeyore on the opposite wall. He wondered if Micah took comfort in it as he drifted off to sleep, or if he was scared of monsters. There was so much Drew needed to learn about his son.

He picked a stuffed dog off the floor, where it appeared to have fallen from the white, wooden crib. He set it inside, where Micah could cuddle it tonight.

Turning, he watched Annie pull on Micah's jeans before tugging a T-shirt over his head. There was some cartoon guy wearing a hard hat on the front.

"He had colic?" he asked, making note of another precious detail. "I've heard it can be bad."

Annie nodded. "It was."

"He doesn't have it anymore?"

"Nope. He turned three months old and it disappeared. Poof. Just as the pediatrician promised. A good thing, because I don't think I could have taken too many more sleepless nights."

"I'm sorry I wasn't here to help." What he wouldn't have given to assist with some of those late-night sessions.

Annie shrugged, stretching to grab a tiny pair of socks from the top dresser drawer while still keeping a steadying hand on Micah. "We got through it."

"But it would have been easier with two of us."

"Drew, it's not like we would have been living together as a family." She propped her hands on her hips. "And it would have been nearly impossible, handing off the baby every other weekend."

He shrugged. "I guess you're right."

Still, he wondered.

Annie deftly pulled one sock, then the other, over the boy's ever-moving feet. "There you go, sweetie. Some shoes and you'll be ready to leave. Drew, would you get the green blanket from the crib?"

"Sure." He grabbed the soft, fuzzy blanket, resisting the urge to bury his nose in it. Already, he loved the kid more than he could have imagined.

What if he isn't yours?

Shaking his head, he wondered if he'd already gone too far down this road to turn back. It felt right to be Micah's dad.

"Come on, let's go before he needs to be changed again." Annie tucked a lock of hair back in her ponytail and straightened her glasses. Then she grabbed Micah and headed for the door.

"Sure thing."

"I've got most of the stuff out front. Let me get some juice and snacks from the fridge."

"All that stuff is going? It looks like enough for a couple weeks at least."

Annie's laugh was infectious. "Spoken like a true amateur. There's a portable playpen in case he wants to take a nap when we get there. Enough diapers to make sure we don't run out under any circumstances. Been there, done that and it wasn't pleasant. Toys. Several changes of clothes and shoes, just in case he encounters water. Which reminds me, are we picnicking near a stream or pond?"

"I've never been to this spot before. My boss recommended it."

"If there's water, we'll have to be extra careful not to let Micah out of sight for even a second. There was another child drowning reported on the news last night."

Drew winced. "I'll watch him like a hawk."

"Good."

Annie stowed a few more items in a soft-sided cooler and slung it over her shoulder. "The diaper bag's out front, too."

"You must really trust your neighbors."

"Ha. Mrs. Washington lives next door. She's better than any security system. And a real sweet-heart, too. She's like Micah's second grandma. My mom's in Payson and she doesn't get to see him nearly as often as she'd like." Annie held out her hand to Micah. "Come on, honey, let's go."

He dodged around her and tried to open the

front door. Fortunately, the round knob was too much of a challenge for his present dexterity. Drew could tell it wouldn't be long, though….

"Remind me to bring some tools next time and I'll install some child safety stuff."

"Already installed." Annie reached up and flipped a small lock at nearly the six-foot level.

"Ah. So Micah can't open the door."

"Right. The little monkey is into everything these days. And to think I couldn't wait for him to walk." She rolled her eyes, but her smile told Drew she loved every minute.

He scooped up the boy. "How about a piggyback ride, buddy?"

Micah crowed, "Piggyback!"

Drew settled him on his shoulders, then grabbed the portable playpen and what seemed like a thousand bags.

Annie picked up the remaining three or four. "All set."

"All this for one afternoon," he said, shaking his head.

Her laughter warmed him.

For a minute, it almost felt as if they were a family.

ANNIE LEANED BACK IN her seat and relaxed. It was sheer heaven not to be driving, to simply allow Drew to take over. And that disturbed her. She barely knew the man and here she was, turning over her responsibility to him.

Still, sharing a bit of the work was a heady relief.

Micah, secure in his child safety seat in the back, pointed out the window and chattered away. His commentary soon slowed to a sleepy word here and there. And the next time she glanced back, he was asleep, his dark lashes dusting his chubby cheeks. In moments like these, she loved him so much it literally hurt.

"He's asleep," she murmured.

Drew glanced in the rearview mirror. "Yeah, that's what I thought. It'll be good for him to catch a catnap before we get there."

"Why down by Tucson?"

"I figured a bit of a drive would give us a chance to talk. Let you get to know me better so you feel secure when I'm with Micah."

She was impressed with his thoughtfulness. He really was trying.

"You said your boss told you about this picnic spot. What is it exactly that you do?"

He seemed to hesitate for a moment. "Right now, home inspections. It allows me to get outside and not be tied to a desk all day. I paid my way through college by working in construction each summer."

"Did you graduate?"

"Business administration. But quickly realized I wasn't cut out for an office job. I've been thinking about going back for an advanced degree."

Annie was about to ask what kind of advanced degree was necessary for home inspections, when she noticed red-and-white flashing emergency lights up ahead.

"I hope it's not a bad accident," she said as they approached.

"Looks like a simple fender bender."

Drew signaled his lane change and they were around the accident in no time.

Annie released a breath. Emergency vehicles still had the ability to set off alarm bells in her head.

Drew grasped her hand and squeezed, the action surprisingly natural, as if this was just one of many trips they'd taken together. "It didn't look like anyone was hurt."

The fact that he could read her so easily should have made her uncomfortable. But it was almost as reassuring as the warm pressure of his hand on hers.

"Um, yes, thank goodness."

Drew squeezed her hand again, then released it.

"We were talking about college. Is that where you learned sign language?"

"I started out at Arizona State, but transferred over to Phoenix College once I decided I wanted to pursue sign language. They have a wonderful program."

"What made you decide on that?"

She'd never confided in anyone about the scare that had caused her to rethink her priorities. She didn't intend to start with Drew.

Glancing out the window, she said, "I'm not really sure if there was one defining moment. I'd gotten tired of the party scene and wanted to focus more on helping people. There was a hearing-impaired girl in one of my classes who brought her own interpreter. It fascinated me from the start."

That much was the truth.

"I imagine it took a lot of hard work."

Annie nodded. "It did. There were times I didn't think I'd ever get the hang of it. It's like learning a foreign language. Only one that requires fine motor skills to boot. Finally, it just seemed to click."

"I bet it's satisfying, knowing you're helping someone."

"It is."

Drew's expression was thoughtful and he didn't seem inclined to pursue more conversation.

Annie took the opportunity to watch the desert unfold through the window and simply enjoy the quiet. It wasn't often she had that luxury these days.

The soft music playing on Drew's radio lulled her. She felt…safe.

Before she knew it, Drew was shaking her. "We're here, Annie."

She sat up, dazed. "I must've dozed off."

"You and Micah both caught some z's."

Self-consciously, she wiped her mouth, hoping she hadn't drooled.

"Where are we?"

"Picacho Peak."

She got out of the truck and stretched. Then she went around to Micah's door. Brushing the hair back from his forehead, she was amazed anew that she'd produced such a perfect child.

"We're here, sweetie." Unbuckling his harness, she lifted him out of his seat.

He murmured something and settled his face against her neck, his breath warm.

"Do you want me to take him?" Drew asked.

"Not until he wakes up completely. He might be startled with a stranger holding him."

She read the disappointment in Drew's eyes. "How long will you consider me a stranger?"

"I didn't mean it like that. He's already getting to know you. Today will help. You just need to be patient…with both of us."

"I hope so," he murmured, grabbing the diaper bag, blanket and picnic basket from the backseat.

Annie glanced around the parking area, which held only two other cars. "There's a trail over there. Is that where we go?"

"Yes. My boss said there's a trail around the curve. Then there's a clearing with a nice thicket of mesquite trees less than a quarter mile away. You're sure you don't want me to carry him? I bet he gets heavy."

"I can handle him," Annie said, as she boosted the sleepy boy higher on her hip. But she had to wonder. When Micah was an infant, she'd carried him in a backpack on the rare occasions she'd had time to hike. With him topping thirty-five pounds now, it put too much weight on her shoulders.

Drew seemed to think better of arguing. "Let me know if you change your mind. This way."

A power struggle averted, they hiked up the trail in companionable silence. The trees rustled in the breeze. Even Micah was unusually quiet, his eyes bright as he took in his surroundings.

Annie breathed deeply, enjoying the fresh air and the warm autumn sunshine. "There's absolutely nothing better than Arizona in the fall."

"Yeah, one of the reasons I never moved back to Michigan after college. My folks have already had snow. They keep threatening to become snowbirds—half the year in Arizona and half in Michigan. Of course, that may become more than talk when they learn about this guy." He cupped Micah's head with his palm.

The tenderness in his expression made her wistful, wishing they'd met under different circumstances. She hoped all the snowbird talk was simply that—talk. Otherwise, she might start worrying about a set of pushy grandparents overrunning her neatly ordered life.

She shifted Micah's weight. He was starting to get heavy. "You haven't told your family about him yet?"

"No. I wanted to make sure I had things straight in my mind before I talked to them."

"And had the paternity test results," she finished, disappointed that he still didn't seem to know her better than that.

"I don't want to get their hopes up, then pull the rug out from under them."

As the trail started to climb, Annie mulled

over what Drew had said as she admired a single orange butterfly making the most of the waning season. It fluttered and coasted, a bright spot of color against the muted sage and brown around them.

She started to see the situation from Drew's perspective. There were so many people who could get hurt if this went wrong. Only she knew the truth.

"Your parents have wanted grandkids for a while?"

"Only forever. And they'd prefer my younger sister finish grad school before marriage and a family. So, yeah, sometimes the pressure is on me."

They rounded the bend and found an ideal picnic spot, shaded by a cluster of mesquite trees.

"It's beautiful," she breathed.

Except for driving to her mom's place in Payson, it had been a long time since Annie had ventured outside the urban sprawl. City parks were nice, but nothing like being in the rugged outdoors. They had yet to even run into the hikers who belonged to the cars in the parking lot.

"How about under that tree?" Drew pointed to a lush area. "It looks like the desert wash isn't running. No water this time of year."

"Perfect."

She followed him and waited while he spread the old blanket.

Micah squirmed to get down. "Picnic?"

Drew laughed. "Your timing is impeccable, buddy. You're like me, any hint of food and I'm wide-awake and raring to go."

Annie set Micah on his feet before kneeling on the blanket next to the picnic basket. "I feel bad. All I brought were snacks and a dessert."

"I told you not to worry about a thing. I figured you'd have your hands full getting Micah ready. Besides, I picked the stuff up at the deli."

Unable to resist, she lifted the lid and peeked inside the picnic basket. The thought of food made her stomach growl.

Micah squatted next to her and looked inside, too. "Brownies."

Annie laughed. "Yes, you and I made brownies, and Drew put them in here. But those are for dessert. We'll have sandwiches first. And it looks like there's some fruit salad in here."

"Sounds like everyone's hungry."

Soon, they each had a paper plate loaded with food.

"How'd you know Micah liked peanut butter and jelly sandwiches?"

"It was a pretty safe bet. It was a favorite of mine at that age and I figured all kids liked them."

"Most. But there's a girl in Micah's class who's allergic to peanuts." Annie didn't want him to think she wasn't grateful for his effort. "But that's extremely rare. PB and J is a great choice."

Grinning, Drew said, "Don't worry, I had a backup plan. There're cheese sandwiches in there, too."

Annie refrained from mentioning that some kids were sensitive to dairy products. And some were lactose intolerant.

"Isn't Be Prepared the Boy Scout motto? Were you an Eagle Scout?"

"No. I had a hard time following rules when I was a kid. The army pretty much forced me to look ahead and prepare for eventualities."

"Was it…bad in Iraq?"

He hesitated. "Yeah, it was."

"I'm sorry. I didn't mean to pry."

"It's okay. They say it's good to talk about it."

"But you're not so sure?"

"It's one of those things where you had to be there to understand." His eyes grew shadowed. He fiddled with his sandwich, but didn't take a bite.

His sadness tugged at her heart. Something terrible had happened to him. His injury?

She picked up one of the cheese sandwiches. "I'd like to try to understand."

He glanced at Micah, who seemed fascinated by a caterpillar crawling across the blanket.

Annie made a mental note to make sure Micah didn't stick the caterpillar in his mouth.

"Drew? We can change the subject if it's too difficult."

Taking a deep breath, he said, "No, it's something I've been trying to face up to."

She pretended to concentrate on unwrapping her sandwich, giving him time to gather his thoughts.

"You know the night we met? I told you I had a hunch I might not make it back?"

She wasn't expecting the intensity of his gaze when she looked up at him. Or how it brought back memories of being his sole focus, if only for a few hours.

"Yes, I remember."

"It wasn't just a way to play on your sympathy."

Annie swallowed hard. That's exactly what she'd been thinking. "It did, though."

"Yeah." His smile twitched as he glanced at their son. "Better than I ever imagined."

She wished he wouldn't act like Micah was a dream come true. It put pressure on her to let him into their lives on a more meaningful basis.

"Your premonition obviously didn't come true." She gestured. "You're here, alive and well."

He stared at the horizon for a moment, his jaw working. "It *did* come true. Every last detail. Except one."

"You survived?"

"Two things then. I survived…and the wrong man died."

CHAPTER SIX

DREW TRIED DESPERATELY not to be sucked in by the memories of that awful day in Iraq. But no matter how hard he tried, he couldn't evade the image burned into his brain.

Orion's playful smirk when he beat Drew to the Humvee seat that was *always* his when the team escorted the chaplain to an outpost.

The shock waves radiating through the vehicle as an IED exploded, sending shrapnel tearing through flesh and bone. The surreal creaks and groans as the Humvee settled on its axles. The choking dust and smoke.

Then, as his vision cleared, Drew saw Orion pinned to the seat by a twisted fragment of metal pipe. Drew was at his side in seconds.

"Hang on, you're going to be fine."

Orion's slight smile told Drew he knew otherwise. "Tell...Beth...I love her."

"No, man, you tell her yourself."

Sweat dripped in Drew's eyes, making them

sting. Or maybe it was blood. There was a haze of red. He wiped his sleeve across his face.

"Not…gonna…happen."

"You can't leave her like this." *Can't leave me like this.*

"Is okay…" His words were slurred. "She's… great."

"She sure is. Beth's one in a million."

"Look…after her."

Drew's throat was raw from dust and acrid smoke. Clearing it, he said, "You can count on that."

"Take…care…of…my guys. *Our* guys."

Orion's breathing grew shallow. His mouth twisted with pain.

"Where's the damn medic?" Drew shouted.

"On his way," Jones called, applying pressure to a neck wound on Gibbs. "Hang on, Orion," he called over his shoulder.

"Drew," Orion whispered.

He leaned closer.

"Gift…is…yours."

"Just stay quiet. Save your strength."

Orion struggled to stand, apparently unaware that he was pinned.

Drew gripped his shoulder and held him still, his heart breaking.

"You…chaplain."

If he could just hold on tight enough, Drew thought, Orion couldn't die. He tried to keep his tone light, so his friend wouldn't know how desperate the situation was. "Now I know you're hallucinating. I'm no chaplain. That's your job."

"Yours."

That was the last thing Orion said to him.

Drew wished he could trade places with the man who was more of a father than his real dad. Wished he could take on his pain as his own.

Pray for me.

He could hear the words as clearly as if Orion had spoken them aloud.

From memories of Bible school long ago, Drew recited, "Our Father, who art in heaven…"

"DREW? ARE YOU ALL right?" Annie asked.

He wiped his eyes, embarrassed that she'd seen him this way. "Yeah. I didn't mean to tell you about Orion."

"He must have been a very special man."

"He was. The best."

Drew glanced around for anything to provide a distraction. That's when he saw Micah and realized what the child had done.

Drew reached out and scooped him up. "Don't eat that."

Annie shot to her feet, holding out her arms. "What does he have? Is it poisonous? Is he choking?"

"Spit it out," he commanded.

Micah's eyes widened innocently.

Drew swept his forefinger in the boy's mouth and held out the wiggling caterpillar for Annie's inspection. "No, not poisonous. But kinda gross."

She paled. "It's not toxic?"

"He'll be fine. The caterpillar should be okay, too, though I'm sure it's in shock."

Drew placed the critter under a shrub far enough away that Micah wouldn't be tempted to go after it. He grasped the boy under his arms and raised him over his head. "No eating bugs. They're yucky."

The kid had the nerve to laugh. "Yucky."

"Micah James, no more eating bugs." Annie shook her finger.

Drew tossed the boy in the air, then caught him.

He was rewarded by more laughter.

"Think that's funny, do you?" He tossed him higher. It only added to the little daredevil's glee as Drew caught him and cradled him to his chest like a football.

He was working up to his third throw when Annie's voice cut through the laughter.

"Drew!"

Turning toward her, he said, "Let me guess. Too dangerous?"

"No. I mean, yes. But he just ate a big lunch. That's not a good idea…"

That was when Drew noticed the kid looked a little green around the gills. He quickly set him on his feet.

"Sweetie…" Annie hustled Micah to the base of a shrub, where he promptly lost his lunch.

Drew was dangerously close to losing his. The day had been a disaster, from start to finish. Not only had he shared his greatest shame with a woman he wanted, no, *needed* to impress, but then he'd managed to make Micah sick.

"I think it's time to go home." Annie's tone brooked no argument.

Drew suspected it would be a long, long time before she would consider him fit to have unsupervised visits with Micah. And at this point, he couldn't really blame her.

ANNIE'S WEDNESDAY LUNCHES with Kat usually pro-vided a welcome workday break, but today she wasn't enjoying the conversation. She glared at her best friend while they waited for the counter person at Someburros to fill their drink order. "What do you mean, I'm being too hard on Drew? The man has no common sense where children are concerned. I've given him opportunity after opportunity to prove he's mature and capable. And every time I think he might be coming around, he does something stupid."

Kat accepted the plastic tray with their drinks and their order number. "I'll grab that booth before someone else gets it. Then you can tell me what you *really* think."

Annie's indignation didn't wane as she made her way to the island to get the utensils and condiments, her job in the division of labor she and Kat had determined long before Micah was born.

After weaving through the crowd of tables, almost every one occupied, she sat opposite Kat. "I'm not being unreasonable. Any mother would be disturbed."

"Okay, I'll agree it wasn't too bright to toss the kid up in the air after he'd eaten a couple sandwiches and a caterpillar...."

A man dressed in a suit at the next table gave them an odd look.

"Shh. He didn't *eat* the caterpillar, he just put it in his mouth."

Kat rolled her eyes. "Whatever. It wasn't life or death. Drew had it under control. And let's face it, disturbing though it may have been, a child vomiting from excitement and rough-housing is not in immediate danger. If he was, there would be a lot more fathers in prison."

"But if those are the stunts Drew pulls when I'm around, just think of what he'll do when I'm not there."

Kat's eyes sparkled with mischief. "There's the William Tell archery game my brothers played with me as a kid. I think I still have a scar on my scalp."

"You're not making things easier."

"No, I'm not. I'm sorry. I'm really not trying to make light of this. But Drew will always be a part of Micah's life. Wouldn't it be better to help him be successful at parenting instead of making the poor guy think he sucks as a father?"

"I *don't* want him to fail." *Did she?*

Just then their food arrived and Annie re-frained from adding any more opinions of Drew's parenting skills.

When the server left with their trays, Kat leaned forward. "Okay, I'm going to throw an idea out here. Have you thought that maybe it's you making him so nervous that he does stupid stuff?"

"Me? I'm one of the least threatening people on the planet."

Kat coughed. "Um, yeah, you can't see your protective mama-bear-side, I guess. It's completely awesome. As long as I'm not the target of all that protectiveness."

"I'm supposed to feel guilty? As if I don't already have enough guilt being a single parent?"

"No, but the guy was sharing a pretty intense personal moment with you—that's a sign of maturity. Maybe you can cut him some slack."

Annie regretted telling Kat about Drew's confession. But she'd been overwhelmed, not sure she'd done the right thing by letting him pretend he hadn't confided about Orion's death. Granted, the caterpillar had been an effective distraction.

She raised an eyebrow, cutting her *pollo fundido*. The aroma of chicken and green chilies made her realize it had been a long time since her hurried bowl of oatmeal this morning. "I suppose you know just how I should do that?"

"As a matter of fact, I have a suggestion."

"Why does that not surprise me? It always seems to be the childless people have the most suggestions about how to raise kids."

Kat's smile faded.

Annie regretted the words the minute they were out of her mouth. "I'm sorry, Kat, I didn't mean that the way it sounded. Especially with your maternal clock ticking."

"No big deal."

But Annie could tell by the hurt in Kat's eyes it *was* a big deal. She was mortified. "You are absolutely the last person on the planet I'd want to hurt. Please forgive me for sticking my foot in my mouth."

Kat hesitated. Finally, she pointed her plastic fork at Annie. "I will forgive you only if you allow me to interfere at will in my godson's life."

"What do you have in mind?" Annie suspected she was being maneuvered.

"Drew mentioned having kind of a flexible work schedule. Since you make him nervous, why don't you see if he might be able to hang out while I take care of the little terror on football practice days? It might take the pressure off both of you. And to be honest, I wouldn't mind the backup. You have no idea how exhausting it is to be the fun godmother."

Not nearly as exhausting as being the responsible single mother.

They ate in silence for a few minutes before Annie ventured, "You'll make sure he doesn't do anything dangerous?"

"Cross my heart. I'll even fill Drew in on the finer points of child care."

Annie suppressed a sigh. It might turn out to be a case of the blind leading the blind.

"I guess…"

"You won't regret it."

Somehow, Annie suspected regrets would be the least of her problems.

DREW TRIED TO IGNORE the hint of nerves as he waited outside Annie's door. He'd been in battle, so he could certainly handle a toddler.

Kat answered the door, talking on her cell phone as she motioned him inside. "I gotta go. I'll get there when I get there…. Yeah, love you, too."

Clicking her phone shut, she said, "Good, the reinforcements are here. He's in fine form this afternoon. Must not have napped much this afternoon at day care, so he's…cranky."

"Maybe he needs a nap now. Any chance he'll watch a movie with me and crash out?"

"Oh, there's a very good chance of that. And Annie'll have my head because he'll never fall asleep at eight tonight. She thinks it's really important for him to have a consistent schedule."

"And you don't agree?"

She shrugged. "Hey, I'm just the babysitter. What do I know about kids' schedules, rigid or otherwise?"

He followed her into the great room, where

Micah watched TV, apparently mesmerized. Drew went over and ruffled the boy's hair. "Hey, kid."

Micah glanced up but didn't smile. "Hi."

Drew went to the breakfast bar and pulled out the stool next to Kat's. "I've been doing some reading and the books recommend a consistent routine."

She rolled her eyes. "Annie's getting to you, isn't she? Next, she'll have you working on a spreadsheet plotting out the next twenty years of Micah's life."

Drew smiled, but felt as if he was being disloyal. "Annie is...meticulous."

"Well, that's why you'll be good for her. Get her to loosen up."

"Is that why you're doing this? Going out of your way to make things easier for me?"

"I'm not doing it for you. I'm doing it for her. And for him." She nodded toward Micah. "Besides, I feel responsible for the whole predicament. I'm the one who had the bright idea to set you two up. Hence, my godson was conceived. Great kid, not so great circumstances."

"Yeah, but I should have had more self-control. And Annie...well, she seemed...enthusiastic at the time."

"But I pushed her to step outside her box.

'Live a little,' I told her. 'Quit fixating on plans and stay in the moment for once.'"

"Hmm. Annie doesn't seem very easily manipulated to me. Did it ever occur to you she was simply overwhelmed by her attraction to me?"

She eyed him up and down. "Don't flatter yourself, stud. You're attractive in a boy-next-door-meets-gym-rat kind of way. But Annie didn't describe it as love at first sight."

He crossed his arms. Didn't women have some sort of code about kissing and telling? "Oh, yeah? How did she describe it?"

"Uh-uh. You'll have to ask her that yourself."

Drew felt a kick to his shin. "Ow."

He glanced down to see Micah glaring at him.

"What was that for?"

Micah kicked him again.

Drew picked him up, mindful not to toss him in the air. "What's got your diaper in a twist?"

"He's just ornery. I warned you."

Chuckling, Drew asked, "How about if we watch a movie together?"

"Thomas."

"Thomas?" Drew raised an eyebrow.

Kat groaned. "Thomas the Tank Engine. We've already watched it once today. And umpteen times yesterday. I think I may lose my mind. But at least he's giving Bob the Builder a rest."

"Why don't I take the next showing?"

"You don't have to ask me twice, Kimosabe. I'll be on the deck if you need me." She headed toward the sliding door. "Oh, and it should go without saying, don't toss or shake the kid. And *don't* let him go to sleep."

"Sounds easy enough." Drew popped in the DVD and settled on the couch next to Micah.

The toddler sighed and snuggled close.

Drew felt the beginnings of a sweet ache in his chest. He stroked Micah's silky hair, more content than he'd ever been. He smiled as he watched his son watch the movie. Micah was enthralled. He repeated dialogue at random and seemed to know it from start to finish.

He glanced at the boy when he stopped repeating dialogue. Micah's eyelids kept closing. His head would bob, then he'd jerk awake.

"Hey, none of that, kid. You're not supposed to fall asleep."

Micah responded by lying down and settling his head on Drew's lap.

Drew stroked his hair. "Tough day, huh, buddy?"

The boy didn't respond. His chest rose and fell with an even rhythm.

Drew didn't have the heart to wake him. He'd just let him catch a five-minute catnap first. That certainly couldn't hurt, could it?

Thomas the Tank Engine and Percy worked together to save the town. Good moral. But not very exciting for an adult.

Drew's head drooped and he jerked awake.

He leaned back against the couch for just a minute....

"Drew, wake up."

He straightened. "I'm awake. I don't sleep on the job. Not when I'm sentry."

Annie crossed her arms over her chest. "You most certainly did."

He wiped his hand across his face. "The heat must've gotten to me today. I didn't hear you come in, and that's unusual."

She shook Micah's shoulder. "Wake up, sweetie. Mommy's home."

Micah murmured something, but didn't open his eyes.

"I hope he hasn't been asleep long."

"Um, no." He glanced at the clock and realized with a shock they'd been out for at least forty minutes.

Kat entered the room. "I thought I heard your voice."

"I walked in and found these two sound asleep.

I'll never get Micah to bed at eight. His schedule's going to be all messed up, he'll wake up cranky tomorrow and it'll go downhill from there."

After seeing Micah in action at the picnic, Drew had a new understanding of how much time and energy it took to single-handedly keep the child safe, let alone happy.

"I'm sorry—"

"*I'm* sorry, Annie," Kat interrupted. "I forgot to tell Drew not to let him fall asleep. It's my fault."

Annie sighed. "Nothing to be done about it now. I was hoping for an early night, and he'll probably be awake till at least eleven."

Drew noticed the shadows under her eyes and felt bad. He opened his mouth, but Kat shot him a glare.

Closing his mouth, he decided he didn't want to lose an ally by seeming ungrateful of her sacrifice.

"I've, um, got some reports to write for work. I better get going," he said. "Should I come by the same time on Thursday?"

Annie hesitated. "I guess so."

Drew was relieved. Time with his son was precious and he didn't want to blow it.

CHAPTER SEVEN

ANNIE TRIED NOT TO GET impatient when Kat wouldn't meet her gaze. Her best friend either had early Alzheimer's or she was up to something. "What do you mean you can't stay for dinner? It's Thursday…you always—You called me not two hours ago to say you'd picked up a frozen lasagna to heat and were going to eat with us."

She tried not to be distracted by the sight of Drew lifting Micah so the boy could sit on the table. The flex of his biceps distracted her, reminding her he was a man's man even when he pitched in with the domestic stuff.

Or maybe he was in collusion with her best friend, who seemed extremely interested in the floor.

"Um, like I said, something came up."

Annie gave up. Anything Kat did was with the best intentions. It was her soft heart that sometimes got her into trouble. "I hope Micah grows up to be as horrible a liar as you."

Kat's eyes widened. "I don't know what you're talking about... I popped that frozen lasagna in the oven about an hour ago, by the way. It should be ready anytime now."

"Thanks, Kat. You're too good to us."

"Of course I am. Now, I need to get out of here. Dillon is pining for my presence." She gathered her purse, keys and cell phone from the breakfast bar. On her way to the front door, she called, "It's the party-size lasagna. I bet if you twist his arm, Drew will agree to stay. No need to waste all that food."

Now Annie was certain she was being maneuvered. "You don't fight fair."

"No, I don't. But it's just one of my many charms." Kat's cell rang as she opened the door. "Hey, Dillon, I'm leaving right now."

When the door shut, the apartment seemed quiet, intimate.

Drew raised an eyebrow. "She's kind of like a whirlwind, huh?"

"Kat is definitely a force of nature. And she's right—it's one of the things I love about her."

"Then I guess I'd better love it, too, because she seems to have taken pity on my starving-bachelor plight."

The thought of Drew sharing a meal in Annie's home seemed too...well, familylike.

But there was no graceful way out. And he *had* been nice enough to rearrange his schedule to be here with Micah. "Please stay for dinner. As Kat said, we don't want the food to go to waste."

"Then I'll accept."

"Good." Annie stood there, transfixed by the unexpected effect of his smile. But then again, his smile had had a similar effect the night they'd met.

And look where it had gotten her.

She forced herself to concentrate. *Dinner. Food.* "Would you mind watching Micah while I pull together a salad and get things served up?"

"Sure." He handed the boy a fork. "We're buds, aren't we?"

Micah crowed, "Buds."

As THEY SAT AT THE dining table tucked away in an alcove in the family room, Drew wondered if dinner would provide more insight into Annie, who, in her own way, was as fascinating as her alter ego, Grace.

Kat had insisted Annie liked to eat casually. The family-style serving and her choice of simple white dishes seemed to confirm it.

Drew watched as she navigated the currents of toddler eating preferences, setting a plastic plate in front of Micah. She'd precut his portion into bite-size pieces. The reason soon became apparent.

Drew picked up Micah's fork, speared a piece of pasta and aimed for the kid's mouth.

"Me do," Micah insisted.

Annie laughed. "Why does that not surprise me? He wants to do everything himself, but I thought he might let you get away with feeding him."

Micah grabbed the pasta from the fork and shoved it into his mouth, smearing sauce on his lips.

"Good for developing fine motor skills, I guess." Drew set the fork down.

"That's what the pediatrician says. But it's hell on my carpeting and tile."

Annie stood and went to the front room, returning with a newspaper. She arranged it on the floor beneath the boy's chair.

"Okay, you do it."

"Is he really *that* messy?" Drew asked.

She laughed, her eyes bright. "You have no idea."

Ten minutes later, he had to admit she'd been right. He had *no* idea.

"Please tell me they learn to use forks and spoons by age two."

"Sorry to disappoint you. Utensils frustrate

him. Looks like it'll be finger foods for a while."

"Maybe he just needs practice. Here, guy, why don't I help you out?" He picked up Micah's fork again.

Micah shoved Drew's hand away and screeched, "Me do!"

"Okay, okay." Turning to Annie, Drew said, "He certainly has strong opinions."

"Yes, he does. Must've gotten it from his father."

"I'm not nearly as outspoken."

The banter made him realize what he'd been missing. What Annie had kept from him. This. The cozy feeling of being almost like a real family. Being a dad to his son.

"This is nice," he said, suddenly feeling anything but nice. He tried to swallow his bitterness as he added, "Having dinner with you two. Thanks for inviting me, even if it was under *duress*."

Annie fiddled with her napkin. "I wouldn't say duress. It's just hard for me…letting someone new in. Someone I don't know all that well."

"So you haven't dated much?" It came out more of a challenge than a question. Drew waited.

"Only once since Micah was born. It was a

disaster. Micah got sick and I had to rush home, and my poor date just didn't seem to get it. That I'd choose to be with my sick child over him. I knew then that it wouldn't work. Maybe I'll try again when Micah's a little older."

Drew exhaled slowly. "Yeah, maybe when he's older."

Like twenty.

He tried to tell himself it was natural to feel protective of the mother of his child. Even though she clearly didn't want him to be the father of her child.

"Thank you for arranging your schedule to be here with Micah today." She passed the glass salad bowl to him. "It makes things easier."

"My boss is a family man, so he understands that I want to spend as much time with Micah as possible. Since I've been with the company for almost ten years—except for Iraq—he trusts I'll get my work done."

He heaped garden salad onto his plate and set the bowl out of Micah's reach. He'd learned quickly.

Annie raised an eyebrow. "You told your boss about Micah?"

"Why wouldn't I?"

She shrugged. "I guess it might be hard to admit. Some people consider it a mistake."

"Was it hard for you when it became obvious that you were pregnant?"

"No. I switched school districts, so nobody knew me from before. The staff was very good to me when I thought…you died. I didn't get specific about our marital status."

It pleased him that she'd been upset when she thought he'd died. Even if she'd cheated his parents out of two years with Micah. He knew the distance wouldn't have kept his mother from her grandson. "I wish it hadn't been that way. If only you'd told me…"

"I can't go back and undo what's been done. I'm sorry, I really am. But it's not fair to keep bringing it up."

He fisted his napkin. He was tired of being fair. "Annie—"

"Excuse me, we need more napkins." Abruptly she stood and went to the kitchen.

Drew thought a sensitive guy would probably go after her, but he wasn't feeling particularly sensitive tonight. Besides, leaving Micah alone with sharp objects didn't seem like a good idea.

She returned almost immediately with a stack of napkins. And he was afraid he could see dampness behind the lenses of her glasses.

He could have kicked himself for making her feel bad. He had to let his resentment go—

if only to help this woman…the mother of his child. "I'm sorry, I didn't mean to upset you. I just get into what-ifs. Things might have been so different."

"How? Would you have rushed to my side to marry me only to leave again and almost get killed? How in the world could that have helped either of us?"

He thought about Beth and how devastated she'd been when Orion died. Somehow he doubted she'd have given up that time with her husband for someone in a safer occupation. But they'd shared thousands of nights together and all the days in between.

"I don't know, Annie. I'm stumbling through this and not doing a very good job of winning you over."

"You don't have to win me over. Just be a good father to our son."

"I'll do my best."

They ate in silence for a few moments. Even Micah curtailed his baby chatter, apparently sensing the tension in the room.

Drew wanted their easy conversation back. The warmth, the give and take.

"I'm glad you stayed in the Tempe area. I've always liked it."

"I thought about moving to Payson to be

closer to my mom, but there aren't as many opportunities there. How about you? Were you tempted to move closer to your folks?"

"They just moved to Oregon. The rest of my family is in Michigan and they really wanted me to move back. But I needed…some space to think things out after I left Iraq. My future, what I wanted to do with my life. Being over there changed my outlook."

"I can imagine," she murmured, her eyes shadowed.

"There were Americans over there who I would have never met otherwise. And we ended up being closer than family. People I would give my life for."

Annie studied him for a moment. "You really mean that, don't you?"

"Absolutely."

She busied herself cleaning Micah's face. It looked like a hopeless task to Drew.

Annie apparently came to that conclusion, too. She sighed and tucked the napkin by Micah's plate.

"Are you going back?"

"I'm not sure. That's one of the things I have to think about. There's so much need over there. Our people, their people."

She leaned forward. "But what about your

parents and everyone who loves you? Don't you have a duty to stay safe for them? Have you thought about how it would destroy them?" Her voice was taut and low.

"How could I not consider my family? I'm hoping they would support me no matter what I decided."

"Even if it meant breaking their hearts?"

Drew shifted in his seat. "This conversation is getting pretty intense. Maybe we should change the subject."

"I didn't mean to pry." But her expression remained troubled as she sipped her iced tea.

Clearing his throat, he asked, "So tell me about your job. Do you work with a group of kids?"

"No, just one. We're kind of joined at the hip during the school day. But I try to give him plenty of room to be a kid and socialize, too."

Drew realized he'd been eating, but hadn't tasted a bite. He consciously slowed down and focused on enjoying being here with Annie and Micah. "Yeah, it's gotta be rough as a teen having an adult with you all day. Not much room for trouble that way, though."

Annie smiled, but she seemed distracted. "Oh, they still try every now and then. But I've been extremely lucky. All my kids have been great. There's a special bond there."

They talked more about her job, his job and how Micah could recite numbers one through ten.

Drew leaned over and ruffled the boy's hair. "You're a pretty smart kid, huh?"

"Me smart." Micah's cheeks bulged with food. Sauce was smeared on his chin.

After a dessert of chocolate ice cream, Drew helped clear the dishes, and prepared to leave.

Annie walked him to the door, Micah on her hip.

"I've gotta go, buddy."

"No go." Micah held his arms out to him.

Drew couldn't believe it. The boy wanted him to stay. Wanted him. He blinked several times. It shouldn't be this way. He shouldn't have to leave his son.

He took the toddler, fully aware of Annie's reluctance to let him go.

"I've got to go home to sleep at my apartment, big guy. That's where my bed is. And you need to sleep here."

Micah wrapped his arms around his neck and hugged him hard.

Kissing the top of his head, Drew found his voice was husky when he said, "I'll see you Thursday. Be good for your mom."

Then Micah let Annie take him.

Drew felt as if his heart was in shreds as he walked away. The trip home seemed to take forever. Probably because every mile he drove took him farther from his son. And Annie.

CHAPTER EIGHT

ANNIE ROLLED DOWN THE windows of her little crossover SUV and inhaled deeply. She glanced at her rearview mirror and stopped herself from commenting on the fresh, pine-scented air.

Micah was asleep.

Her plans for the weekend trip to her mother's place in Payson had been made a month ago, so she shouldn't feel guilty over Drew's disappointment about not seeing his son today. But she did.

Annie negotiated the turn where paved road changed to dirt. The handy Tucson took it in stride, though. They arrived at the A-frame cabin right at noon.

Her mother was outside raking pine needles, looking younger than her fifty-six years in slim jeans and a fisherman's sweater. Probably pretending she hadn't been waiting for them.

Annie smiled. If motherhood had brought about changes in her, being a grandmother had caused June Marsh to bloom.

Her mom had the rear passenger door open almost before the vehicle came to a stop.

"Come here, you angel. Let Grandma give you a big hug."

Micah viewed her through half-raised eyelids. "Gramma," he murmured, breaking into a smile.

A smile that was reflected in her mother's eyes. It was a love affair that had started from the moment Micah had come home from the hospital.

Annie got out and went to give her mother a hug. "I see how I rate."

"Oh, honey, I'm so glad to see you. But you know I just couldn't waste a second before I gave this little one a hug." She took Micah out of his safety seat and did just that, placing noisy kisses on his neck.

"I know, Mom." Annie draped her arm over his mother's shoulder as they headed toward the cabin.

"How was your drive?"

"Uneventful."

June opened the screen door and headed for the eat-in kitchen. "I've been holding lunch for you two. I made sub sandwiches for us. PB and J for Micah. And macaroni salad. Oh, and brownies for dessert."

"You've hit all his favorites. He'll be one happy kid."

"He's always a happy child. That's how I can tell what a good job you're doing."

Annie appreciated the attempt to bolster her confidence, but wished her mother wouldn't lay it on so thick.

"Thanks, Mom." Annie felt the tension of the past few weeks ease.

"Every parent needs to hear they're doing a good job. But you really are. And maybe later you'll tell me why you've seemed…distracted when I talked to you on the phone. That way *I'll* feel like a good parent."

"There's something I need to tell you about Micah's dad. But let's wait till after lunch."

Her mom raised an eyebrow, but refrained from asking the questions that seemed to be on the tip of her tongue. Instead, she put Micah in his booster seat at the old, battered oak table and placed enough food for three children in front of him.

Annie wished she could avoid the conversation that was coming. She hated to spoil what would have otherwise been a perfect day.

DREW UNLOCKED THE DOOR and walked into his apartment. Glancing around, he tried to see it as Annie might if she came to his place. It looked generic, from the inexpensive rental furniture to the lack of personal items. He'd obviously made no effort to turn it into a home.

But he was about to remedy that in a small way. Kill two birds with one stone, so to speak.

Taking the digital picture frame out of the box and packing, he set it on the kitchen table next to his laptop. Then he began downloading the photos he'd taken of Micah when he'd babysat on Thursday. There was even one that Kat had taken of the two of them. He'd e-mail it to his folks, too, when they got the all-clear on the paternity test.

He was still amazed this kid was his son. But Micah looked too much like Drew to be anyone but a Vincent. The cleft in his small chin clinched it. And, within the next week or so, they would have DNA confirmation from the lab.

The phone rang and he picked up, the display showing a private caller.

"Hello."

"Hey, it's Kat."

"Hi. Is something wrong?"

"No. I just need to ask a favor."

"Shoot."

"Brett's coach called an extra practice on

Monday and I told Annie I'd babysit, but I realize I've got a doctor's appointment. Any chance you could fill in for me? You're definitely ready to go solo."

Drew felt a little sheepish that he was pleased to hear he wasn't a total moron with his son.

"Sure, no problem. As long as it's okay with Annie."

"I'll clear it with her. I tried to call her cell, but she must be out of range. Reception can be kind of spotty by her mom's cabin. I left a voice message, but thought I'd line you up so Annie wouldn't have to worry about it late Sunday when they get home."

"Do I need to pick Micah up from preschool?"

"I imagine Annie will phone you Sunday night with the details. But if you have any questions, feel free to give me a call."

"Okay, Monday afternoon. Got it."

"Thanks, Drew."

He clicked off his phone and stared at his computer screen, bemused. He was going solo on Monday. The thought both excited and scared him.

In an attempt to distract himself, he started downloading photos from Iraq. But emotions and memories flooded him with each picture.

Good people, good friends. They'd taught him so much. First, how to survive in a war zone. And second, that some bonds were too strong to break simply by distance.

Or by death.

His favorite photo of Orion flashed on the screen. Standing against the tan, desolate landscape of Iraq, the older man was grinning broadly, backing up, his arm cocked to throw a football to an unseen serviceman. He was vibrant, with an unparalleled zest for life. But even that hadn't been enough in the end.

ANNIE TUCKED MICAH INTO the crib next to her mom's bed, then tiptoed into the kitchen. She selected a dish towel and started to dry while her mother washed. There was no room in the tiny A-frame for a dishwasher.

Annie was just as glad there wasn't. There was something soothing about their after-dinner ritual.

"Is he asleep?" her mother asked.

"Yes."

For some reason, the repetition of drying made it easier for Annie to think. And talk. "You remember when I told you Micah's father had been killed in Iraq?"

"Yes. It was so sad."

"Well, it turns out he's alive. He was wounded badly, but survived. As a matter of fact, he made a full recovery."

Her mother didn't speak for a moment, just scrubbed the same pot even though it was already clean. Annie started to wonder if she'd heard her.

Finally, June said, "I bet that was a real shock. Do you…intend to contact him?"

"Turns out, he contacted me."

"I don't know what to say, Annie. I've grown so accustomed to thinking of Micah as ours and nobody else's. I know that sounds selfish, but there you have it."

Hearing her own emotions spoken aloud made her ashamed. And caught her off guard, coming from her progressive mother.

"I have to admit, I'm surprised." Annie dried her hands and started putting the dishes away to make room on the counter. "You're normally pretty inclusive."

"This is my grandson we're talking about. Not to mention this man let you go through a difficult pregnancy by yourself and didn't try to contact his son for more than eighteen months. As far as I'm concerned, being dead is the only acceptable excuse." Her mother's cheeks flushed with anger.

Annie felt ashamed, but she had to own up to the truth. "Drew didn't know about Micah."

Her mother stared at her, trying to process that.

"He contacted me to…apologize."

"For what?"

"The whole one-night stand thing. Apparently his conscience started to bother him when he was overseas. But it wasn't his fault. I was…a willing participant."

"It does generally take two to dance that dance. But it doesn't let him off the hook from his responsibilities."

"He, um, wasn't even sure Micah was his child."

June frowned, scrubbing at a stubborn spot. "I don't think I like this Drew."

Annie separated the utensils and placed them in the appropriate slots in the silverware drawer, finding comfort in the routine task. Her voice was low when she said, "I really messed things up. First by having a fling, then by convincing myself there was no need to confirm that Drew had died. I can't really blame him… for wondering."

"I can. You would never be intimately involved with two men at once. Even though certain matriarchal societies find it acceptable."

Annie had to smile. "Did you ever…? On second thought, don't answer that. You grew up in a different generation. Free love and all that."

"I was in love with your father when I was very young and monogamous and devoted to him. But I also believe there should be options. It's a shame women seem to be losing all the ground we made in the sixties and seventies. The pill freed us. Fear of disease has shackled us again."

"For all your talk, it's not like you replaced Dad with a bunch of guys."

"No. I was too damaged at the time. I've had a few male friends since. Sex is a healthy communication tool. And it's just downright fun."

Annie rolled her eyes, wondering why she couldn't have one of those mothers who never discussed anything remotely intimate with her daughter. But deep down, Annie considered herself lucky, even if all this openness sometimes made her squirm.

"Um, I'm not real sure what Drew and I were communicating when we had sex."

"That you needed human touch. That maybe you were a tiny bit lonely? That you were still young enough to throw caution to the wind?"

"Were?"

June pointed at her with a wooden spoon covered in suds. "You know what I mean. These days, you're so intent on being the perfect mother you've shut down that part of being a woman."

Annie snorted. "It's not like I have a ton of opportunities. Besides, I tried dating and it doesn't work. Not while Micah's so young."

Her mother tilted her head. "Maybe it doesn't work because you haven't found the right man yet."

This was another familiar refrain, and only served to make Annie sad. Her mother had an idealized view of male-female relationships, formed around a man who would stay forever thirty-nine in her memory. Annie had pretty much given up on the fairy tale.

"Can we change the subject? Tell me about your work at the clinic."

"Okay, I'll butt out of your sex life for now. The clinic is fine. We're doing good work there. Important work. Women need control over their reproductive rights."

Annie smiled, admiring her mother's zeal. She also found it ironic that she'd had an unplanned pregnancy when her mother had preached responsible, safe sex to her practically from the cradle.

"I'm glad it's going well, Mom."

"So is this Drew interested in seeing Micah?"

"He has seen him. He's also been helping out after school when I'm at football practice with Brett."

"He doesn't have any crazy idea like wanting custody, does he?"

"He understands that it's important for Micah to get to know him slowly. We haven't really discussed visitation."

"You should consult with an attorney, all the same."

"Now you sound like Kat."

Her mother wiped the last dish clean and dried her hands. "It's only because we love you, honey. And love Micah."

"I know." Annie sighed. "I hope you're wrong. I can't think of anything much sadder than two parents fighting over a child. I don't think there can be a winner that way."

CHAPTER NINE

ON MONDAY, ANNIE DASHED across the parking lot, up the stairs, and unlocked her apartment door. Once inside, she set Micah on the floor. They were home an hour earlier than usual. That would give her time to hyperventilate before Drew arrived. Or call Coach and say she was sick and couldn't attend practice.

"Snack?" Micah asked.

"Of course, sweetie." She went to the kitchen and got a juice box and some of his favorite fish-shaped crackers.

She glanced at her watch, so tempted to make that call.

But she'd have to give Drew time alone with Micah eventually. And none of the other interpreters had been able to cover for her.

There was no way she could take Micah with her to the practice, she couldn't divide her attention between a toddler and the coach. And letting down Brett was not an option.

Grabbing a couple of Micah's trains, she held out her hand to him. "Come with Mommy? You can play trains while I check something on the computer."

Micah complied and quickly settled on her bedroom floor to play.

Annie's conscience twinged as she booted up her PC. But she decided Micah's safety was more important than Drew's privacy.

She opted for the least expensive search available that would include court records. If he had a felony, her decision would be made and Brett would have to be disappointed. An ex-wife? She'd be forewarned. A current wife? She'd know he couldn't be trusted.

Working quickly, she referred to the social security number he'd given for the DNA test, while telling her conscience to be quiet.

The file downloaded quickly—showing no marriages, past or present. That cheered her immensely.

No criminal record. Woo-hoo!

Saving the file, she decided there was really no reason not to let him babysit. Kat said he was a natural.

As for Micah, he adored Drew. Annie wondered if the child knew on some instinctive level that Drew was his father. Or if he was just starved for male companionship.

"Okay, sweetie. Let's go clean up the family room."

"Game."

"Yes, bring your trains."

He followed her to the front room, where they began the cleanup game. They sang and danced around the room as they placed all the toys in the storage box.

Before she knew it, the doorbell rang.

Annie was breathless when she opened the door. "Hi, Drew. Come on in."

For some reason, she felt unaccountably shy. Maybe it was because his hair was still damp from a shower and he smelled great. Or maybe it was simply because he was the only man she'd been intimate with in six years.

Over halfway to double digits. Life was passing her by at an astounding rate.

"Hey, buddy," Drew said as Micah hugged his knees. He swung the boy up in his arms, without tossing him in the air.

Annie nodded in approval.

"Do you always get off this early?" he asked.

"No, I took an hour of personal time to pick him up at day care."

"I could have picked him up."

Giving permission to the day care for one day seemed…complicated. And she hadn't wanted to give permission for Drew to pick up Micah because it might seem as if they shared custody. That was a precedent she didn't want to set.

Drew held her gaze. "He's my son. It wouldn't have been a bother."

"You don't have a safety seat for him, do you?"

Snapping his fingers, he said, "I didn't even think of that. I'll buy one on my way home tonight. That way I'll be ready next time."

Maybe there wouldn't be a next time. "Kat doesn't have these appointments often."

"Even so, I'd like to do it more. It's good for me to get to know Micah." He tousled the boy's hair. "And we have fun, don't we, buddy?"

"Fun!" Micah crowed.

Annie was reluctant to have Drew as a regular fixture at their place. "We'll see."

She glanced at her watch, then grabbed her purse and keys from the breakfast bar. "I've got to go. You be a good boy."

Kissing Micah on the cheek, she blinked away unwelcome tears. Why was this so hard?

Drew touched her shoulder. "We'll be fine. I've got your cell number if we need you."

Nodding, she turned and left before she cried in earnest.

DREW TIPTOED AROUND pots and pans and the small human cyclone that had emptied the cupboards. The same cyclone who sat happily beating on an upended pot with a long-handled spoon.

"Easy there, Micah, we don't want the neighbors complaining about noise."

The boy grinned and drummed louder.

Drew felt a headache somewhere behind his right eye.

"You can do this," he reassured himself. "You've been in battle."

The first hour had been a piece of cake. They'd laughed, they'd played, they'd read books.

But then Drew had the bright idea of having dinner ready when Annie got home to show he really had this dad stuff down pat.

Once he'd started, Micah had morphed into a whiney, demanding, energetic bundle. As a last resort, Drew opened the lower kitchen cupboard and turned him loose. And like thousands of children before him, Micah was able to entertain himself with basic cooking tools.

Drew grabbed plates from the upper cupboard and set the table, including toddler utensils for Micah. Not that the kid would probably use them.

Stepping around Micah, he opened the oven door a crack to check on the macaroni and cheese casserole. It bubbled, the top turning a golden brown. And it smelled pretty darn good, too.

Out of the corner of his eye, he saw a small hand reaching out to the oven door.

"No!" he yelled, pushing Micah's hand away.

Startled, the toddler started to wail.

Drew shut the oven door and turned down the heat so the casserole would stay warm.

"Shhh. It's okay, buddy."

The wail turned to a screech.

Crouching next to the boy, he said, "I didn't mean to holler. I was scared you'd get burned."

But Micah wasn't listening. Great tears rolled down his face onto his pint-size polo shirt.

Drew picked him up and cuddled him close. "It's okay. I'm not mad. You're fine. I didn't mean to yell."

The screeching lowered a decibel, but the neighbors probably still thought someone was being murdered.

Just then, he heard the front door open, and Annie dashed in, her eyes wide.

"Micah." She ran to the kitchen and wrenched the boy from Drew's grasp. "What's wrong, sweetie?"

"It's nothing."

"Mommy," Micah sobbed, wrapping his arms around her neck and holding on for dear life.

"It's okay," Drew stated. "I just startled him."

Annie's gaze swept the room, taking in the apparent explosion in the kitchen. "Shhh, honey, it's all right," she crooned.

Micah's cries magically subsided to a hiccup or two.

She glared at Drew. "What really happened?"

"He's fine. I opened the oven to check on the casserole, and saw him make a grab for the door. I didn't want him to get burned so I guess I yelled, and he got scared and—"

"Hey, slow down."

"—he started crying."

"He does that when he's scared. I imagine he's tired, too. But otherwise he seems fine." She checked both chubby hands and kissed each in turn.

"You believe me?"

She hesitated. "Yes, I do."

"Whew. I was afraid you'd think the worst. That I'd screwed up again. Or that I'd hurt him."

Smiling slowly, she glanced around in wonder. "Congratulations, you passed your first big test. Trying to prepare dinner with a toddler underfoot. It smells wonderful, by the way."

"Macaroni and cheese. Homemade. My mom's recipe."

"Well, then, let's get dinner on the table." She set Micah on his feet, swatted his behind and started putting away pots and pans. "I'll get drinks if you handle the casserole. And I think I've got a bagged salad in the fridge."

"Sounds like a plan."

Passing his first parenting test was nearly as fulfilling to Drew as coming back from his first mission in one piece.

They sat down to dinner and he cleared his throat. "Do you mind if say the blessing?"

Annie blushed. "Please, go ahead, if you'd like."

He grasped her hand in his and leaned across the table for Micah's.

Annie pulled back as soon as Drew finished.

Glancing up, he was surprised to see that her eyes were watery.

"Hey, did I do something wrong?"

She turned her face away. "No, um, I just remembered some of the dinners with my dad and…sometimes I still miss him."

Drew didn't know whether he should press for details. How in the world did he think he could be a counselor when one teary woman reduced him to a mass of indecision?

"Do you…want to talk about it?" There, that was a relatively safe response.

Slowly, she faced him. "My dad was big on having dinner together as a family. After he…died, I used to wish he could come back for just one more meal, so things could seem… normal again."

"I had no idea. I'm sorry."

"It hits me out of the blue sometimes. You'd think after a couple decades I wouldn't have these flashes of missing him."

"Hey, I've seen some of the bravest men cry for their mom or dad when they were hurt. It's nothing to be ashamed of."

She wiped her eyes and smiled. "Thank you. Now, let's have some of that casserole. Did Micah tell you it was his favorite?"

"I think he might have mentioned it. At least ten or twelve times."

Drew let her change the subject, tabling the many questions he wanted to ask about her father. She obviously didn't want to talk about it anymore, and he had to respect that. For now.

KAT CALLED LATER that evening, after Micah was bathed and in bed.

"So?" she asked. "How did it go with Drew?"

Annie leaned back on the couch and sighed. "It went...well."

"You don't sound sure. What happened? Did he make the kid puke again? And here I was positive he could handle it."

"He did fine."

"Then why aren't you happy?"

Good question. Where Drew was concerned, nothing seemed clear-cut. Least of all her emotions.

"He did *too* well."

"And that's a bad thing because?"

Annie hesitated. "Because I...liked him tonight."

"Oh, honey, you are in such trouble. He's in the reserves, and I've heard they can be called up at almost any time. You have the hots for him, don't you?"

"No, absolutely not. It was all very innocent."

"Oh." There was a world of disappointment in one syllable.

"But you know what? He had dinner ready

when I got home, and we ate together. That's our second dinner in less than a week. We seemed kind of like…a family. A dad, a mom and a kid. And it was…magical."

"It scares me to hear you refer to him as magical. But I think Drew being successful at this is good for all of you. No matter what happens, you guys will be tied to each other through Micah. And if you get along, nobody needs an attorney. It's a win-win."

Annie wiped her cheek, surprised to find it was wet. Taking a deep breath, she said, "Um, yeah."

"You sound funny. Are you crying?"

"No!"

"Yes, you are. What gives? I'm your oldest and dearest friend and you should confide in me."

"It's nothing, really."

"Tell me."

"You wouldn't understand."

"Try me."

Kat was more tenacious than Micah angling for a cookie right before a meal. She would never give up.

"Dinners weren't the same after Dad died. Mom and I just grabbed a bite to eat whenever. She was messed up the first couple years after he was gone, and half the time she wouldn't have eaten at all if I didn't make her. I used to dream about my dad walking through the door and having dinner with us at the table, saying grace and the whole nine yards." Annie stood, walked to the window and stared into the night. "Tonight I had that. Or something that seemed so close."

"Aw, honey, you always seem so together about losing your dad. I forget how hard it must've been."

"My whole life changed. I adored my father. So did my mom. It was as if the light went out of her, like her body was there, but her spirit went with him. Sometimes I wonder if it was because she watched him fall."

"But your mom eventually made a new life."

"Yes, she has the clinic and her causes. And now she has Micah. But you never knew her before. She was… phenomenal. I've always wondered if I could love that fully. I wonder if it was worth it to her when she lost him so young."

"I bet she would say it was. Why don't you ask her?"

Annie went back to the couch and sat with her legs tucked beneath her. "I don't want to dredge up the past. Especially now when she finally seems to be getting over it."

"Promise me one thing?"

"What's that?"

"You'll give Drew a chance. You won't shut him out because you're afraid of getting close."

"That's a stretch, even for you, Kat. Just because we seemed like a family for a few minutes doesn't mean I intend to get romantically involved with him. And he hasn't said he wants to pick up again, either."

"Everyone deserves a happily ever after." Kat's voice softened as she added, "Especially you."

CHAPTER TEN

DREW SAT ON THE FLOOR and played cars with Micah. There wasn't anywhere he'd rather be on a Thursday afternoon.

"You're gonna be a gearhead, I can tell already," he told his son. He maneuvered his stock car around the crash Micah had engineered, complete with sound effects.

Kat snorted from where she sat on one of the bar stools. "Not if Annie has anything to say about it. Too dangerous."

"Yeah, she said something about wanting him to be an accountant like you. I still have a hard time seeing you as an accountant."

"Why? I'm a very methodical person."

As if to demonstrate her point, she pulled a bottle of nail polish out of her purse on the breakfast bar, carefully aligning the bottle with cotton swabs and some other stuff Drew couldn't identify. She shook the nail polish, then started to apply it with the precision of a machinist.

"I can see that." He gestured to her shoulder-length riot of auburn curls, peasant blouse and toenails painted a vivid red. The same color she was now painting her fingernails. "I'm sure you are. You just seem too… free-spirited for that line of work. Too…outspoken."

"I'm a wallflower at heart."

"Uh-huh. And I'm Jimmy Johnson."

"Jimmy who?"

Drew scoffed in disgust. "The race car driver."

"Sorry, we free spirits don't follow car racing. We're too busy slacking."

"I didn't mean it that way." Drew sensed he needed damage control and pronto. "It was a compliment. Accounting is just kind of boring to me. You're more action oriented. Vibrant."

Her eyes narrowed. "Vibrant, huh? I guess I'll let you off the hook then. And for the record, I enjoy the predictability of accounting because my life can sometimes be very… unpredictable."

Nodding, he said, "Makes sense. So now I understand that you are a multifaceted woman."

Micah made a crashing noise and rammed Drew's car.

Drew laughed. "Boy, I better get some good insurance when you're old enough to drive, kid."

Micah found that uproariously funny. He jumped up and down while he imitated Drew's booming laughter.

"Little ham."

Drew turned to Kat. "I haven't begun to figure out Annie."

"What's to figure? She's always been a straight shooter, with this really cool, quirky side she only shows to the people closest to her."

"Maybe her quirky side was coming out the night we met. I almost didn't recognize her when she answered the door a couple weeks ago. She's a lot more…uptight."

Kat blew on her nails, then started applying polish to her right hand. "She's got a child to consider now. She wants to be the best mom ever."

Drew thought about it as Micah continued the game of demolition derby with their cars. He loved the kid's enthusiasm. Drew had been the same at his age, or so his mom said. Usually she followed it up with a comment about how many gray hairs he'd given her.

"I get the idea there's more going on with her than that. The night I met her, I thought she had the most amazing contradictions. She was sexy, yet innocent. Funny and warm and beautiful and smart…."

"She still is funny, warm, beautiful and smart. And I'm not just saying that because she's my best friend. But I encouraged her to step outside of her box that night, live a little. Be more like me, I guess. It was a dumb idea and it ended badly."

"Not all that badly." Drew glanced meaningfully at his son. "I can think of at least one good thing to come of it."

"Now everything's okay, but you weren't there when she was sick and in danger of losing him. Her pregnancy was scary and not just because she was alone. She grieved when she thought you'd been killed."

He hesitated. "I didn't realize. She never said anything." He was comforted to find out that he'd meant something to her. She'd been this wonderful enigma to him. A puzzle that he'd mulled over when the reality of war got to be too much.

"It's hard for her to be reminded that she stepped out of line after she'd sworn off men. But believe me, she grieved."

"Sworn off men?"

"Uh-huh."

"How long?"

"I've already told you too much. You'll have to hear the rest from her. I just didn't want you to think she didn't care about you."

"Thanks. It…means a lot."

"Just don't hurt her, okay?"

Drew was saved from responding by Pink's "You and Your Hand" coming from Kat's purse.

"You changed your ring tone."

She shrugged. "I call it my man-hating music. I'll just let it go to voice mail."

"Boyfriend's in the doghouse?"

"Yes."

Kat hesitated for another few seconds before she pounced on her purse, and had the cell to her ear before the last tone. Turning away, her conversation was a low murmur.

A few moments later she said, "I've gotta go. Tell Annie I'm sorry, something came up and I won't be able to make it to Max's party."

"Max's party. Got it." Drew didn't like the tight lines around her mouth. He'd come to think of her as a friend and he looked out for his friends. He stood to walk her to the front door. "Are you okay?"

"I have to go bail the jerk out of jail. I'll be fine after I kill him."

Drew shook his head as Kat blew a kiss to Micah and sailed out the door. He would never understand why otherwise sane women fell for losers.

ANNIE UNLOCKED THE DOOR, calculating how quickly she could change her clothes for the party. She prayed Kat had Micah ready to go. That way they could arrive a few minutes early and leave early.

Drew met her at the door, carrying her sweaty son under his arm like a sack of potatoes.

She kissed Micah loudly on the cheek, his giggle melting her heart. It almost made her forget the aroma of grimy little boy.

Drew set him on the ground and he scampered away.

"I take it he hasn't had a bath yet?" Annie raised an eyebrow, fighting to hang on to her good mood.

"Kat didn't say anything about a bath. She had an emergency. Bailing some jerk out of jail. Said she was sorry, but she'd miss Max's party."

Annie groaned. "Let me guess—Dillon?"

"Whoever has her angry-woman ring tone."

"Dillon. My guess is another DUI charge. If the guy worked as much as he parties, he'd be damn near solvent. It figures he'd mess up when I needed her most." Sighing, Annie said, "I hate going to these things alone. I need backup, tonight especially. I'd beg off, but Micah would be disappointed."

"What kind of backup?"

"Have you ever been to a two-year-old's birthday at the Party Palace?"

"No, that's one pleasure I've missed."

"Consider yourself lucky." She shuddered. "Noise, sugar and overstimulated children— not a good combination."

"I take it Max is a two-year-old?"

"Yes. And not just any two year-old. The most rambunctious toddler I've run across. But maybe I'm prejudiced because his parents are so horribly condescending about 'poor Micah' and how hard it must be to come from a broken home."

Drew crossed his arms over his chest, his frown downright forbidding. "I haven't heard that term in a long time. I imagine Kat would set them straight."

Annie grinned. "At the very least she would have assured me just how normal I am, and a wonderful mother."

"I could do that."

Annie liked the way he said it without thinking, without hesitation.

"I appreciate it. But how do I introduce you? Your presence might be hard to explain."

"Maybe we could start telling people I'm his

father." He held up a hand before she could protest. "I realize I insulted you with the way I asked for a paternity test. There was absolutely nothing about you to suggest you were promiscuous. It was just my stupid, knee-jerk reaction."

Annie swallowed hard. She'd desperately wanted him to believe it without the benefit of a lab test. But panic outweighed her long-awaited vindication. "The time isn't right. We don't even have the test results yet."

"I know he's mine." Drew stepped closer. "The family resemblance is too obvious. The test is just a formality now."

Annie felt hemmed in with him standing so close. As if he sucked all the air out of the entryway. "I'd better get Micah ready."

She moved past Drew into the great room, where a makeshift fort had been constructed in the corner out of blankets.

Micah emerged from it, grasped her hand and pulled her toward it. "Fort!"

"Time for a bath, sweetie."

Spying his cars on the coffee table, he went over and picked up his favorite, running it along the back of the couch, making *vroom-vroom* sounds. Annie tried to focus on the moment and not the clock. She desperately wanted to preserve him just as he was right now—when she was the center of his world, the only parent he thought he had.

But that was selfish and she'd only be cheating him in the end. He and Drew both deserved the chance to develop a solid bond as father and son.

Still, her pulse pounded at the thought of telling Micah. She wasn't ready yet. How would she explain it so a toddler could understand?

Stalling, she said, "Micah should have time to process the idea before we make it common knowledge. I don't want to do the wrong thing and scar him for life."

"I'll give you a few days," Drew said. "But I want to sit down with you later this week and discuss a time line."

Annie busied herself picking up toys and putting them in the big box. She handed Micah his favorite stuffed bear. "Honey, would you go put this in your room? I'll be there in a second."

Micah hugged the animal tightly and headed off down the hallway. For once, he didn't argue.

"Annie? Are you going to answer me?"

"There's no time line for this. It's a matter of responding to Micah's needs."

"His needs or yours?"

Annie bit her lip, unwilling to make the concession he needed. "He'll be back in the room any second and I don't want to discuss this in front of him, no matter how carefully we choose our words."

"When *will* we discuss it?"

"I know you don't owe it to me, but please give me more time?"

"I don't want to miss a minute more. He needs to know I'm his dad."

"Shh." She nodded toward Micah as he came down the hallway from his bedroom, a cowboy hat pulled low over his eyes. He crawled into the fort again.

Annie stepped closer to check out the construction. "Chairs and blankets. Why didn't I think of that?"

"Maybe it's a guy thing." Drew shrugged. "That's his Indiana Jones hat. Believe me, Indie won't be listening to a word we say. He's too busy looking for treasure and bad guys in the cave."

"Indiana Jones? How does he know about Indie?"

"I rented the movie. He loved it."

"That's got to be PG-13. Inappropriate for a toddler."

Drew sounded wounded when he said, "I covered his eyes during the scary parts."

Planting her hands on her hips, Annie seized upon what he'd said, aware she was only postponing the inevitable. But she was desperate.

"Did you ever think to ask me if it was okay to show him that movie? Did you ever think I might have kept that kind of junk away from him for almost two years for a reason? That one of my more important jobs as a mother is to keep him from exposure to risky or violent behavior? And then you casually pop it in the DVD player like it's the most natural thing in the world."

"It's not like I was showing the kid porn or horror flicks."

Annie was so angry she could barely contain it. "I don't want him growing up thinking weapons and danger are cool. I want him to embrace empathy and kindness and tolerance."

Drew ran a hand through his hair, pacing a step or two. Then he swung around, his eyes bright. "You're so wrong if you think shielding him from life will make him a better, more sensitive man. I felt more empathy and kindness from my buddies in Iraq than I would have in any number of touchy-feely Mister Rogers's neighborhoods. These men and women admitted they were afraid at times, but they always came through, and I knew they had my back. They knew I had theirs. There is no greater empathy than that. Using a gun doesn't change it."

Annie looked down at her shoes. Drew's passion surprised and shamed her. "I'm sorry, I had no idea. Obviously, we've got a lot to talk about in deciding how our son should be raised."

His throat worked as he got his emotions under control.

She touched his arm. "I'm sorry. I didn't mean to start an argument."

The lie almost choked her. He was getting too close, too soon. Too possessive of Micah. And it scared the hell out of her.

His stiff posture told her she'd crossed a line.

"Please, can we have this discussion later when we're both calmer?"

"Yeah. I better go." He started toward the fort in the corner, presumably to tell Micah goodbye.

"Drew?"

He halted. "What?"

"Will you go to the party with us?" It was as much of an olive branch as she could muster at the moment.

"Because you feel guilty or because you want my company?"

"Both." She raised her chin. "And I'd kind of like you there as backup."

"Fair enough. But don't think the subject is closed."

"I know better."

Annie suspected she had only seen a trace of Drew's passion. And the thought both terrified and intrigued her.

CHAPTER ELEVEN

THE PARTY PALACE WAS unlike any place Drew had ever been in in his thirty-three years. He felt as if he'd landed in the twilight zone. The noise was deafening, nearly as bad as a mortar attack.

Laughing, shrieking children ran everywhere. Bells and sirens rang on games. And a few kids, probably as on edge as Drew felt, stood on the sidelines, crying.

Drew had the feeling he might want to join them by the end of the evening.

Annie glanced at him, raising an eyebrow, as they stood surveying the chaos. "Don't say I didn't warn you."

"I thought you were exaggerating."

But Micah's face was transformed with delight. He tugged on Annie's hand. "Let's go!"

Drew chuckled at the child's infectious joy. Suddenly, he saw the huge room through his son's eyes and it became an exciting adventure.

"This way," Annie called over her shoulder

as she followed the sign that read Barton Birthday, with an arrow under it.

Adventure aside, he was grateful to see several private rooms. He was even more grateful when they entered the Barton room and the noise level dropped by at least three decibels.

"I'm so glad you could come." A trim, blond woman patted Micah's head. "Max is over there. Why don't you go join him."

Micah didn't have to be told twice. He dashed off to see his friend.

No hanging back or social anxiety for his kid.

"Hello, I'm Kara."

He shook hands with her. "I'm Drew."

Kara raised an eyebrow expectantly, as if prodding him to explain his relationship to Micah. Or Annie.

But Drew had no intention of falling into that trap. Annie stepped forward. "I'm sorry I forgot to introduce you. Drew is an old friend of mine."

He tried not to wince. It made him feel like an unwanted tagalong. A pity date.

"Yes, well, welcome."

"Thanks. Where do you want this?" He nodded to the large, gaily wrapped package he carried.

"On the table over there. Then feel free to find a seat anywhere. They should be bringing in the pizza any minute now. The cake will be after the games."

"Thanks, Kara." Annie nudged him toward the loot table. She followed close behind.

It was amusing to see her out of her element. At the apartment, she was the undisputed expert on all things Micah.

She rearranged packages to make room for theirs on one of six long, rectangular tables. "Can you believe the excess?" she whispered. "It's not as if one child can ever play with this many toys."

"Lucky Max."

She snorted. "Hardly. The rule of thumb for kids' parties is one guest for each year of age. Max is two, hence two guests. How many kids do you think are here?"

Drew surveyed the room. "Twenty-five or more."

"You're probably close. Not only did Kara invite Max's entire preschool class, but also the class next door—because she didn't want any hurt feelings."

"So she was being considerate. That's a problem how?"

"She was not being considerate. She's showing off and it's a bad example for Max."

"I agree it's a little over the top, but what's the harm—"

"You'll see." Annie adjusted her glasses.

It was almost as if she expected Max to sprout horns while his head made a three-hundred-sixty-degree rotation.

"I think that guy wants us to join him." Drew nodded in the direction of a dark-haired man waving them over to a table near the front of the room.

"Damn. I guess we'd better get the cross-examination over with."

Drew felt decidedly underdressed as he surveyed the guy's suit and tie while they wended their way among the tables to reach him.

He stuck out his hand and Drew shook it. "Bob Barton. You must be Annie's new boyfriend."

Drew felt Annie stiffen beside him.

He decided the less he said, the better. "Drew Vincent."

"Annie, don't you just look beautiful."

"Hi, Bob."

The man enfolded her in a crushing hug. He held her just a fraction longer than necessary and he had damn near leered at her when commenting on her appearance.

Drew had the urge to make some sort of possessive statement like, "Get your hands off my woman." But he suspected Annie would deck him or lecture him. So he kept his mouth shut.

"Sit down, you two. The table of honor." Bob's hearty laugh grated on Drew's nerves.

"Annie, don't you think we should sit closer to Micah, in case he needs help with his food?"

She threw him a look of pure gratitude. "Of course."

But Bob held up his hand. "Now, don't be a hover mother, Annie. This is a time for the kids to cut loose. And the parents to chat."

Even though he agreed in principle, Drew's instinct was to defend Annie. His expression must have been transparent, because Annie leaned closer and squeezed his arm, warning him to play nice.

He recalled her saying something about Kara being a fellow interpreter. Annie's work life might suffer if he didn't mind his manners. "Um, yeah, we'll sit down. But we'll still want to keep an eye out for Micah."

Bob clapped him on the shoulder. "Good man. It's about time Micah had a male role model. It's not healthy for a boy to just be around women."

Annie turned her head a fraction, so Drew was the only one to see her roll her eyes. He was surprised she didn't reach out and smack Bob upside the head.

As it was, Drew was itching to. The guy kept staring at Annie's chest.

"Um, yeah, role models are important. Annie does a great job on her own, though."

"Defending your woman." Bob slapped him on the shoulder again. "I like that."

"So do I." Annie's smile was deceptively sweet as she tucked her hand in Drew's arm. Drew wondered if Bob knew how close he was to annihilation.

Drew surreptitiously glanced at his watch as he sat. Two more hours of this. He was damn near nostalgic for the honesty of barracks life.

Just then, servers streamed into the room carrying pizzas.

The kids cheered.

The adults sighed with relief.

Drew caught Annie glancing regretfully at a table closer to the children, where a lone couple dared to be labeled overprotective.

A smart thing, too, when midway through the meal, Max climbed on the table and did an impromptu tap dance in the middle of a pizza. Then started flinging that pizza at his guests. The couple halted the ensuing food fight by disarming him and his second in command, a redheaded tyke, and pulled Max kicking and screaming from the table.

Bob got up and barreled over. "Take your hands off my son. There's no need for that. He was only having fun."

Drew bent his head and murmured in Annie's ear, "If I'd have done something like that when I was a kid, I wouldn't have sat down for a week."

Annie grinned. "That was then. Nowadays, parents use time-outs instead."

"Yeah, good luck with that." Drew nodded toward Max, who had escaped his captor and was racing around the room, screaming at the top of his lungs. "Of course, my parents had the sense to limit my soda consumption, too."

"Oh, but Bob would think that was stifling Max's fun."

Drew enjoyed the shared moment. They were a team, if only for the evening.

Then a warm little body wedged itself between them.

Micah, his eyes wide, scrambled up to sit on his mother's lap.

"Poor guy's overwhelmed, huh?" Drew asked.

"I was afraid of this."

"He's safe here between us."

The stiffness eased from Annie's posture. "Yes, he *is* safe."

Man, he could get used to this.

ANNIE UNLOCKED HER APARTMENT door, opening it wide for Drew to carry in a sleeping Micah.

"Thanks, Drew. He's much harder to pack around than when he was an infant. You'd think I wouldn't need to go to the gym." She laughed self-consciously.

"Yeah, he's deadweight," Drew murmured, following her to Micah's room. "But you don't need the gym, Annie. You're fine just the way you are."

As far as compliments went, it was understated at best. Yet she still felt pleased. "Thanks. It's nice to hear."

"Not that I was looking at you that way. I just wanted you to know that having a baby hasn't changed you."

She grinned. "Okay, I'll accept that as a compliment coming from a friend. And you get points in the empathy column."

"Whew, that's good. I sure need them."

She didn't want to disturb their truce by revisiting the Indiana Jones infraction.

Drew nodded toward the dresser. "If you'll pick out some pajamas, I'll wrangle him into them."

"He'll need a clean diaper, too, I'm sure. I doubt it will wake him—he's completely zonked out."

The truth of what she's said was confirmed when Drew placed Micah on the changing table and the boy didn't even twitch.

Annie got a lump in her throat as she watched him maneuver Micah out of his clothes.

Had her father taken such tender care of her at the same age?

She glanced up to find Drew studying her.

"I'll go get a washcloth." She escaped his scrutiny and returned with a warm cloth to bathe Micah's face, neck and hands. By that time, she'd regained her composure. "He really needs a bath, but this will have to do."

Drew held out his hand for the cloth. Somehow, she was reluctant to relinquish it. As if by giving up this intimate task, she was giving up custody of her child.

Shaking her head, she let him have it before it was too cool.

She tried not to watch Drew, but couldn't seem to stop. Amazing, how a man so strong and masculine could be so gentle.

It brought back disturbing memories of how sweet his hands had felt on *her* body almost three years ago. And made her long to feel them again.

Annie turned so he wouldn't see her confusion.

When he tucked Micah into bed, Drew was smiling. The love she read in his eyes intensified the ache in her chest. She didn't know if it was for what she'd lost as a five-year-old when her father had plummeted down a mountain, or for the partner and soul mate she couldn't allow herself to look for.

She kissed Micah on the forehead and tucked the blanket more securely around him.

"I better go," Drew said, heading out of the bedroom.

She closed the door behind her as she followed, disturbed to realize she didn't want him to leave.

"I think a glass of wine is in order first. It's the least we deserve after that fiasco called a party."

He grinned. "I hate to admit it, but I'm a little on edge."

"You hide it well."

"Being a soldier is as much about mental resilience as physical. Fake it till you make it."

"If you say so. Have a seat and I'll pour the wine. It's a white zinfandel. I hope that's not too sweet for you?"

"I'm not much of a wine drinker, so I'm sure it'll be fine. A change of pace."

"I wish I could offer you a beer…."

He leaned against the kitchen counter. "I'm not much of a drinker at all these days."

She raised an eyebrow. "You managed to knock back a few beers that night we met. Pre-flight jitters?"

"Yes and no. If I was in a bar back then, I drank. But my jitters had more to do with you."

"Me? Really?" Annie couldn't help but smile at the thought. "I made you nervous?"

He accepted the glass of wine, but didn't move toward the living room. He seemed comfortable in the kitchen.

She leaned against the counter beside him, taking a sip of her wine.

Drew swirled the wine, but didn't drink. "You made me nervous because I couldn't quite figure you out. Now I know why the clothes didn't quite match the vibes I was getting. They weren't yours."

"What vibes were those?"

He hesitated. "That you weren't a quick-fling kind of woman. It meant something if you slept with a man."

"But I did have a quick fling with you," she pointed out, refusing to be let off the hook, no matter how badly she wanted absolution.

"And you cried afterward. I sure could've

used a drink then. I felt like such a jerk. Even worse when you took off without saying anything."

Annie's cheeks warmed. "I'm sorry. I…I'd made a promise to myself that I wouldn't be impulsive where men were concerned, and was upset that I'd broken it. What would you have said if I had stayed?"

"Probably a lot of postsex B.S."

"Figures." She was vaguely disappointed by his answer, but admired his honesty, anyway.

He reached over and fingered a lock of her hair. "But I sure as hell would have asked for your phone number and e-mail address. It would have been nice to have someone else to write to."

"You would have? I thought you'd forget all about me once you got over there."

"Not likely. I thought about you all the time." His gaze was intense. "Some days, that was all that got me through."

She'd meant something to him. He hadn't seen her as just some military groupie or one-night stand.

She would never let him know how much it meant to hear him say it. "You're not just trying to get in my bed again, are you?"

His grin sent a charge straight to her heart.

"The thought of being in your bed again is downright tantalizing. But no. I'm not."

"I'm curious. Why'd you think about me? I'm sure you've had plenty of women." Long-legged, gorgeous women who didn't cry after having perhaps the most phenomenal sex of their lives.

"If I closed my eyes I could smell the scent of your shampoo, feel the texture of your skin…" His voice lowered to a sexy growl. "See every beautiful inch of your body."

His words brought it back in vivid detail. So vivid that her breathing grew shallow, her pulse raced.

When she could speak without sounding like an idiot, she said, "Um, I don't think this is such a good idea."

"No, probably not. I thought you should know, anyway."

Annie took another sip of her wine, resisting the temptation to gulp it down.

"Drew, can I ask you a question?"

"Yeah?"

"I noticed you're not drinking your wine. I hope I didn't put you on the spot…if you… have a problem with, um, alcohol." She rushed to assure him, "It won't make a difference, but…it's supposed to be hereditary."

He shifted. "I'm not an alcoholic. But I've avoided excesses of anything since I got back from Iraq. Because I've heard of too many guys self-destructing when they got home. I don't intend to do that."

"I'm glad," she said softly.

Annie was afraid of how much she cared.

CHAPTER TWELVE

DREW WAS STILL WIRED when he got back from Annie's house less than an hour later. Their conversation had changed course after her admission that she cared. And neither quite knew what to do with that.

He was more grateful than he would ever admit. It took most of the sting out of her unrealistic parenting expectations.

How would she react if she realized how serious he was about becoming career military? Not because he necessarily agreed with everything in the military, but because it was where he was needed?

Funny, knowing he had a son should have made him less willing to consider becoming a chaplain. But in some ways, it left only one clear choice. He wanted to be so much more than he was, for his son. For Annie.

Drew shook his head, amazed at the changes in his perception.

Flipping open his laptop, he switched it on. Sure enough, there was an e-mail from his buddy Twitch. The kid got the nickname from having a nervous twitch the first three months he was in Mosul. But he'd settled down and Drew had trusted him with his life.

Twitch had volunteered for a second tour and Drew wished he'd been there to talk to the kid, see where his head was at and if his decision was more than a knee-jerk reaction.

As Drew read the e-mail, it was almost as if he was in Iraq. He could feel the grit that coated every surface and worked its way into every orifice. Could smell the stench of raw sewage and rotting trash so common in some Iraqi cities. And see the night sky, a blanket of stars sparkling in the inky blackness, reminding him that it was, as the song said, one world.

He shifted in his seat, resolving to send them more baby powder in the next care package.

He shot off a response to Twitch, chuckling. Drew wished he could tell his buddies and family that he had a son.

Soon.

Very soon.

ANNIE HEARD LAUGHTER as she walked into the apartment on Friday. It sounded like Kat and Drew, with Micah's giggles thrown into the mix.

Her smile froze as she entered the great room and saw Drew on the floor, intertwined with her best friend while Micah danced around them.

Annie saw red. And it wasn't the large red dots on the vinyl sheet.

Micah saw her and shouted, "Mom!" He raced over and she grabbed him up in a hug, burying her face in his neck, inhaling his sweet, salty scent.

When she looked up, she figured the ache in her chest matched the blue circle where Kat's rear end rested.

Annie cleared her throat. "It looks like you guys are having fun." So much fun that it was hard to tell where Kat's legs began and Drew's ended.

"Twist her," Micah pronounced, clapping his hands.

"I can see that."

"When did you get here?" Drew asked, standing. He held out a hand to Kat and helped her up.

Annie wanted him to release Kat immediately, if not sooner.

"A minute ago." There, her voice sounded almost normal.

"It seems like forever since I've seen you."

Kat, in jeans, brushed imaginary dust off her perky butt. At least Annie figured it looked perky to Drew, judging from the way his gaze lingered on it.

Annie couldn't believe how childish she felt. This was her best friend, Kat. And Drew.

She'd made some bad choices in men, though. They'd all seemed honorable. Until they revealed some big old relationship buster kept carefully under wraps. Like Jeff's wife. Or Ron's delight in driving after a few drinks, speeding around curves on a deserted mountain road.

Annie's throat went dry as she recalled the sickening squeal of metal on metal as the guardrail buckled. The stark terror as she climbed out the driver's door after the crash and knew one wrong movement could send the car plummeting into an abyss. Ron's laughter, as if they hadn't been inches away from death.

The memory had faded over the years, but not her simmering resentment of men who couldn't or wouldn't act like adults. Men who thought relationships came a distant second to an adrenaline fix. It was what fueled her determination to know a man inside and out before she slept with him. Until Drew, that is.

"Hey, what's wrong? You have a bad day?" His concern should have reassured her. She was really starting to like him. And that's what worried her.

He stared at her expectantly.

Kat's eyes narrowed.

Annie released a breath. "Yes, I had a bad day. The quarterback got the wind knocked out of him and couldn't get up. After that player in Chandler who was paralyzed, it makes me sick when something like this happens."

"The boy is okay, though?" Drew asked.

"Yes. He's fine."

"Good. I can only imagine the hell I put my mother through with my sports. Football, wrestling, racing motorcycles…"

Kat folded the vinyl Twister sheet and put it in the box. "You raced motorcycles? Cool."

"Don't ever encourage Micah to do something like that."

Drew touched her shoulder. "Annie, he's going to find his own interests. And probably a few of them will result in bumps and bruises. That's all a part of growing up."

"I'd love to stick around for this debate, but Dillon's driver's license was revoked so I'm designated driver one hundred percent of the time." Kat grabbed her purse from the breakfast bar.

"That sucks," Drew commented. "I guess you managed to forgive him."

"Yes, it sucks and yes, I forgave him. That reminds me, we have a meeting with his attorney tomorrow and I know you have a game, Annie. I hate to bail on such short notice."

"An attorney on Saturday?" he asked.

"Yep, DUI attorneys seem to work 24/7. I'm sorry, Annie."

"I don't think I can find anyone to fill in for me this late." She turned to Drew. "Is there any chance…you might be able to sit with Micah?"

"On one condition. You let me bring him to the game. We'll be in the stands, but we won't bother you. It's been ages since I've seen a high school game. And Micah will get a kick out of the crowd and band and stuff."

She sighed. "Put that way, I guess I can't refuse. Just cover his eyes if anyone gets hurt, okay?"

"I promise."

DREW MET ANNIE AT the field before the game started. They'd driven separate vehicles in case Micah got restless and Drew needed to take him home early.

"There's your mom, buddy." He pointed her out from the sidelines. Holding the child on his hip, he strode over to the low fence separating the spectators from the field.

Annie glanced up and saw them, her smile making him catch his breath. If she'd been a sexy siren the night he met her, tonight she was sexy in an entirely different way. Smart, sweet and confident in what she was doing.

"Hi, you two. I'm so glad you're here."

"Mom!" Micah, fortunately, wasn't bent on being in her arms. Maybe he'd understood Drew's explanation that Mommy was working, so the guys were going to hang out together.

"Where's Brett?" he asked. "I feel like I know the kid."

She pointed. The teen was a little on the scrawny side, but apparently was a very good punter. He was in conversation with one of his teammates.

"You're right, he does seem to speak well. Not as much for you to do, huh?"

"It's still important to be here and confirm the coach's instructions."

"We'll go find a seat and let you get back to work." Drew raised and waved Micah's arm. "Say goodbye to Mommy."

Micah snatched away his hand to prove he could wave just fine on his own. His independent streak never ceased to amuse Drew.

They went up the bleacher stairs. Bob and Kara Barton waved. There were seats available next to them, but Max was there, too, and Drew wasn't eager for a repeat performance of the birthday party.

He smiled and nodded, pretending he didn't notice the seats.

They kept going three more rows to where Drew spied more seats before Micah spotted his friend.

Micah was enthralled when the marching band came on the field. After a short musical interlude, they took their seats in the bleachers not far away. The other team's band did the same, sitting on the opposite side.

Drew was fascinated watching Annie do her job. Her fingers flew, a blur against the navy blue background of her shirt and pants. Her black-rimmed glasses gave her that geek-girl look he found totally hot.

The game started off well, but Micah fussed after the first quarter. Drew reached into their soft-sided cooler and brought out the carrot sticks Annie had packed, along with juice boxes.

But the boy pointed at popcorn, then cotton candy. "Me want."

"I know you do, buddy." As a matter of fact, the smell of nachos wafting from a few seats away made Drew's stomach growl.

But even if he could circumvent Annie's dietary strictures, the logistics of getting food from the booster club booth back up the bleacher stairs, all the while keeping track of Micah, were too complicated.

So he helped himself to a carrot stick. "Mmm, that's good."

Micah's glance all but said, "Who do you think you're fooling?" He pushed the bag away.

"Me want." He pointed again at the cotton candy. What kid wouldn't want bright purple-and-turquoise swirls of sugar? They fairly screamed of a trip to the dentist and novocaine.

"No way. Your mom would be really mad at me."

"Me want." He stuck out his bottom lip, usually the precursor to a temper tantrum.

"Let's watch the game. See, Brett's going out to punt the ball."

But Micah would not be distracted.

Drew was resigned to packing up and leaving, when a soft, familiar voice said, "Drew Vincent, I didn't expect to see you here. Who's your little friend?"

Beth sat in the seat next to him.

He didn't know what surprised him more, seeing Beth at the game or seeing her in jeans and a team sweatshirt. "I forgot Damian made the team. This is my…friend…Micah. I told you about him." He gave her a warning glance.

She seemed to understand. Extending her hand to the boy, she said, "Any friend of Drew's is a friend of mine."

Micah eyed her hand.

"Shake it," Drew prodded in a whisper.

Micah's expression was serious as he reached out and gave her a very adult handshake. Then he became momentarily distracted by the panther mascot gyrating down on the field.

"I thought I'd let you know that Mac—from your unit—will be home on leave next Thursday. I'm going to have a barbecue in his honor a week from tomorrow. I know he'd want you to be there."

Drew grinned. "I wouldn't miss seeing that S.O.B. for anything in the world. Pardon my language."

Beth laughed. "I've heard worse. Even said a few things I wasn't proud of. Little pitchers have big ears, though." She nodded toward Micah. "Why don't you bring him and his mother to the barbecue? Micah could play with my granddaughter and the other kids."

Drew was sorely tempted. It got old going to parties by himself. He felt like some grizzled bachelor, unable to persuade a woman to marry him by age thirty-three. Truth was, he'd never wanted to ask any of the women he'd dated to marry him.

But now he felt lonely. He'd changed. First, from having his world turned upside down in Iraq. Then, finding out he was a father.

"So how about it?" Beth tousled Micah's hair. "Will you bring this guy?"

"I'll ask his mom. Thanks, Beth."

"Great. I best get back to my seat now. I bet my granddaughter ate all my popcorn."

Drew felt as if his life was finally making sense. As if he'd been waiting to be a family man.

It would be good to see Mac again. And show off Annie and Micah. Not that he could claim either of them as his own.

Yet.

CHAPTER THIRTEEN

ANNIE TURNED DOWN HER car stereo so she could unwind and think on the way home. Practice had run long and she was keyed up.

Her weekend had been uneventful except for the game. Kat had been busy carting her boyfriend all over the place, so she wasn't around. Annie's mom had been in town, but was involved in some women's reproductive health rally way over on the northwest side, and she and Micah hadn't even seen her.

She'd loved being with her son. Sometimes she envied stay-at-home moms. But after forty-eight hours of being around only a toddler, she'd longed for adult conversation.

She'd even considered calling Drew. How crazy was that? She suspected he'd have been happy to spend extra time with his son, but she just hadn't been able to reach out to him.

He scared her on so many levels. The fact that he was Micah's father and could make a claim for joint custody wasn't as frightening as it had once been. She trusted him. And the realization stunned her. But quick on its heels came the knowledge that there was an undercurrent of danger with Drew. His experiences in Iraq had left a deep impression, one she suspected might run deeper than he let on. And that left her with a lot of unanswered questions. Like, had he found the adrenaline rush addictive?

Annie didn't do unknowns anymore.

Which made her attraction to Drew all the more disturbing.

It wasn't only a physical attraction, though her body had been emphatically reminding her that it had been a long time since she'd been with a man. And in her dreams, she remembered in vivid detail just how awesome it had been with Drew.

How was she going to face him at the apartment without replaying the dreams in her mind? And how in the world could she keep him from detecting her thoughts when her face was an open book? Not for the first time, Annie wished she was a better liar.

Pulling into the lot, she parked her car beneath one of the canopies reserved for residents. She squared her shoulders as she got out, hoping Kat would provide a buffer.

Annie listened intently as she let herself in the front door. All she heard was the low murmur of Drew's voice. The smell of cooking food enveloped her as she went into the great room.

There she found Micah ensconced in Drew's lap, looking through his baby book.

"That's you, buddy, when you were only a day old." Drew pointed to one of the photos she'd carefully labeled.

"Me?"

"Yep, it sure is. You were such a tiny thing."

Annie raised an eyebrow. "Tiny is a relative term, even with preemies. Believe me, they call it labor for a reason."

Drew and Micah looked up. Their smiles were identical and both warmed her heart, for very different reasons.

Annie set her purse on the coffee table. "Where's Kat?"

"Where else? Driving her low-life boyfriend around."

Annie chuckled. "We agree on that. I keep telling her she has to start dating men who actually deserve her."

"Too bad. She's a great person."

Annie felt a pang of jealousy, but muzzled it quickly. Drew and Kat had become friends over sharing babysitting. Kat had reassured her after the Twister episode, even though Annie had insisted she didn't need reassurance.

"I've got lasagna in the oven," Drew said. "Should be done in about ten minutes. I thought maybe we could discuss…that *topic* after dinner. Maybe plug in a movie for Micah?"

"I didn't have lasagna or the ingredients. What gives?"

"I brought it, compliments of Mama Stouffer. I figured if I was going to invite myself to dinner, providing the meal was the least I could do."

Annie was impressed with the gesture. She just wished they didn't need the discussion.

"Thank you. I don't suppose you brought a movie, too?" she teased. "Extreme Fighting?"

"As a matter of fact, I did bring a movie. The newest *Veggie Tales*. I figured I couldn't be accused of corrupting him with that."

"You never cease to amaze me."

"Good. That means you'll never get bored with me," he said, winking.

Annie wasn't quite sure how to take that, so she said, "I'll go set the table. It's only fair since you made dinner. Even if you did invite yourself."

The meal was a relaxed affair. Annie had grown accustomed to having Drew around, and enjoyed sharing tidbits about her day and vice versa.

"Have you always been an inspector?"

"Ever since college. I worked my way through school picking up odd construction jobs. After I graduated, I wasn't sure what I wanted to do. I only knew that a nine-to-five desk job wasn't for me. One of the general contractors I worked with suggested I talk to a buddy of his about inspecting. I did and that's how it began. But before I left for Iraq, I had applied for the police academy."

Annie felt the blood drain from her face. "Police? Did you…pursue it since you got back?"

"No, it didn't seem like a good fit." He shrugged. "I'd like to help people in a less confrontational way."

"I'm glad to hear it. You've got Micah to consider, after all."

He nodded. "I've thought long and hard about how my career choices may affect Micah and my relationship with him. I don't want to jeopardize that."

She released a breath. "Home inspections sound nice and…safe."

"Danger can be relative. I could be hit by a bus tomorrow. Or slip in the shower."

Micah's spoon clattered across the table. Annie intercepted it without missing a beat and placed it near her plate, out of Micah's reach.

"Yes, but what are the chances? I'm glad you decided not to become a policeman. I'd worry a lot less about you falling in the shower than getting shot in the line of duty."

"You'd worry about me?"

"Of course I'd worry. You're the father of… well… you know what I mean." She glanced at Micah, who seemed absorbed with his dinner.

Drew reached across the table and took her hand. "I thought maybe it meant you cared."

Annie swallowed hard when a bite of garlic bread refused to go down. "I care, okay? Don't make a big deal out of it."

"Me want." Micah stretched to reach his spoon. She distracted him with a piece of garlic bread, hoping he'd forget about the spoon.

"I guess I'll have to be content with that. For now."

Pulling her hand away on the pretext of drinking from her glass, she wished her emotions weren't so muddled.

Tilting his head, Drew said, "I still want to give back, but in a different way. It feels like I've turned my back on my friends overseas. It seems like I should be doing more."

Annie's heart started beating double time. Surely he couldn't be thinking of going back? If police work wasn't fulfilling, then being cannon fodder wouldn't be so great in the grand scheme of things, either.

Something stopped her from asking him. Maybe she was afraid of what he would tell her. She chose her next words carefully. "I imagine there's a certain amount of…adjustment for everyone once they return."

"Absolutely."

"You'll settle in." Settle down was what she meant.

"Maybe." He didn't look convinced, though. "I keep thinking there's more that could be done to prepare the guys before they ship back."

"I imagine…it's important."

"It was a pet project of Orion's. He wanted to see more chaplains in the field, so they could counsel the soldiers more before they got back. As it is, it's about all they can do to put out fires over there. The divorce rate is high and the strain on a family is phenomenal."

"I don't know how they manage. I'd be a nervous wreck." Annie leaned over to wipe Micah's face with her napkin.

"No!" Micah shook his head, trying to evade her. Some days he was so contrary it seemed as if he was already well into his terrible twos.

"How do spouses deal with the constant worry, never knowing if that call is going to come? It was hard enough when I barely knew you and saw your name on a list. I'm so glad you're back safe and sound."

"Yeah. Me, too." But he couldn't quite meet her gaze. "And maybe they believe in what their husbands or wives are fighting for. Or maybe they just hang on to faith. A soldier needs every bit of family support he can get. In essence, the spouse is in the service, too. The better-adjusted soldiers are usually the ones with a strong support system back home."

Annie had the feeling he was trying to tell her something, that there was a subtext here she didn't want to face. She resolutely ignored the alarm bells. "Did I tell you how well Brett did on his Algebra test? I was so pleased for him."

Drew didn't seem to mind that she'd changed the subject. As a matter of fact, he appeared relieved. While serving himself another helping of lasagna, he asked the appropriate questions about Brett.

After dinner, they both cleared the table and Annie loaded the dishwasher, while Micah generally got under foot.

"Hey, buddy, I've got a great movie for you to watch."

Micah clapped his hands and hopped in place. "Indie."

Laughing, Drew swung him up in the air. "Oops, I forgot. No going airborne on a full stomach. No, the movie is not Indiana Jones. You'll like *Veggie Tales*, though. I've read that kids your age love it. Come on, let's go plug it in."

Annie smiled as the two trooped off to the great room. She wiped down the scarred table and the laminate counter, more content than she'd been for a long time.

She poured herself some wine, loving the way the zinfandel shimmered through the crystal glass—a Christmas gift from Kat one year. Then Annie refilled Drew's water glass.

He returned a few minutes later and she gestured for him to sit at the table. "I gave you water. But if you'd prefer a glass of wine, I can get it."

"No, water's good." He shifted, seemed almost reluctant to sit.

Uneasily, Annie sat first and he finally took the seat opposite.

Drawing a deep breath, she asked, "So is this about the time line?"

"Yes, I'd like us to tell Micah this weekend."

Annie hesitated. "I've been putting it off because I just don't know what to expect. I mean, how do we tell him so he'll understand?"

"Probably as simply as possible. As he gets

older, he'll ask more questions. We'll follow his lead and be as honest as possible."

She smiled. "When did you get to be so smart about kids?"

He shook his head. "Lots of reading. And spending time with Micah. I'm starting to feel comfortable, like I know what makes him tick."

"It shows. You're really good with him. How about if we tell him on Saturday?"

"Perfect." He drank almost half his glass of water. "There's something else. I'd like Micah to spend the night at my apartment Saturday. Get used to the lay of the land. Maybe pick out some things for his bedroom. I sure am glad I opted for the two-bedroom floor plan. Who needs an indoor gym, right?"

Annie shifted in her seat. "He's never spent the night away from me. Not even at my mother's, and he adores her. I don't think so."

"Won't you at least consider it? You're going to have to let go eventually. If you show him you're okay about the visit, it won't be a problem."

Annie swallowed hard. The panic was back, as if she were underwater, fighting for air. "I can't. Not yet. Please understand?" She started to reach for him, but then let her hand drop.

"It's hard to be patient when I've missed so

much. The younger he is when he makes the transition, the easier it'll be."

"I'm trying to adjust, really I am. But this is new to me, too. I thought you were dead. Sharing custody never entered my mind. And now, you're already asking me to hand off my son for a night."

Drew ran his hand through his hair. "I know. And I appreciate it. If I give you more time, will you do something for me?"

"What?"

"I've been invited to a family barbecue Saturday afternoon. One of my buddies is home on leave, and Beth, Orion's...widow, has invited me."

"It's important you reconnect with your buddies."

"She invited you and Micah, too."

"Why would she do that?"

"She knows I've been hanging out with you guys."

"You didn't tell her about Micah, did you?"

His guilty flush told Annie all she needed to know. How could he betray her like that?

"This is how you keep it under wraps? By telling your service buddies?" She stood, unable to contain her agitation.

"Shh. Only one person." He pulled her arm. "Sit down. Please?"

Annie sank into her chair.

"Beth is special, like a mother to me. I needed to talk to someone right after I found out... and...well... I was confused and excited. Orion's the one who would have helped me with something like this. She was a link to him."

Annie thought about it for a moment. Would she have been able to keep such big news from Kat? The way he'd described Orion, the men had been almost family. Her pulse rate dropped and so did her anger. "He was special, too."

"Yes. The best."

"I guess I can understand. I'd probably do the same thing in your shoes." Annie grinned guiltily. "I'd tell Kat right away and swear her to secrecy."

"Beth won't tell anyone. But I would like to be able to tell my buddies Saturday night. I promise I won't, though, if you're not sure."

Annie hesitated. Her heart went out to Drew. He hadn't asked for this strange situation any more than she had. He was a good guy doing the best he knew how.

"I'll think about it, all right?"

"And will you and Micah come with me? Whether I'm able to claim him as my son or not."

"I don't think that's wise."

He rubbed her forearm with his thumb. She'd forgotten he was still grasping her arm.

"Let me think about it for a minute, okay?"

"I'll try not to rush you."

She sipped her wine. The music from the movie drifted softly to her ears.

If she gave a little on this issue, maybe he would be more willing to compromise in the future.

And it would be the perfect way to keep an eye on him and make sure he didn't tell any more than she was prepared to allow.

"We'll go."

"Thank you." He hugged her quickly. "This will be so great. You won't regret it, Annie."

She stepped back. "I haven't decided whether we should make it common knowledge that soon."

"You guys will meet some of the most important people in my life. It's still great. Thank you."

Annie tried not to get caught up in his eagerness. She would do what seemed prudent for her son. Micah's welfare came first and foremost.

Always.

CHAPTER FOURTEEN

DREW WAS NERVOUS ON Saturday when he arrived at Annie's door.

What if she'd changed her mind about telling Micah today?

He clenched his teeth. Then he'd just have to persuade her otherwise. This was too important and he'd been patient.

Shaking his head, he could almost hear Orion's voice.

Easy does it, son.

Drew knocked and was able to appear reasonably calm when Annie answered.

She smiled and invited him in, but seemed on edge. She never stopped moving and her hands flitted as she talked. Even so, she was gorgeous. Her hair looked as if she'd used a curling iron or something on it to make it wavy.

"Micah's in his room, waking from a nap. I listened on the monitor and heard him chattering to his stuffed animals. He's been looking forward to seeing you. Looking forward to the barbecue, too, though he has no idea what it's all about."

Drew held her by the shoulders. "Hey, this is going to be okay. The two of us should be able to handle any questions one toddler can throw at us."

She nodded. "Thank goodness he's not old enough to ask details about the reproductive process."

"Please tell me that's at least fourteen years away?"

"Not hardly, buster. It's recommended to start with simple explanations by the time they start school."

"Then we've got a short reprieve." He paced a few steps. "Should we get this out of the way?"

"I guess so. I'll go get him."

Annie returned about five minutes later with Micah perched on her hip. The boy's cheeks were rosy and his hair tousled. When he saw Drew he stretched out his arms.

Emotion welled up in Drew's throat, making it difficult to swallow. He loved this little guy like he'd never loved anyone before.

"Hey, buddy," he said as he reached for his son. "Let's go hang out on the couch. Your mom and I want to talk to you."

"'Kay."

Drew carried him over and sat down. Micah laid his head against Drew's chest. Closing his eyes, Drew just wanted to revel in the moment.

He felt the couch cushion dip as Annie sat next to him. Still, he kept his eyes shut, breathing in the scent, enjoying the moment.

It wasn't more than two minutes later when Micah began to squirm. Drew loosened his grip and the child climbed down.

Opening his eyes, Drew watched him pick up his favorite toy car.

Annie tucked her hand in Drew's and squeezed. "Those moments aren't as frequent these days. I savor every second because he's turning into a big boy and soon my baby will be gone forever."

The understanding in her pretty blue eyes was almost Drew's undoing. This sensitive stuff was tough. "It's hard to let go when I've just found him."

"I know."

"I've heard some pretty brave guys call for their mothers when they were injured."

"You said that earlier. Let's hope we never have to put that to the test with our son."

"Our son," he murmured. "That's the first time I've noticed you calling him that."

"Is it?"

"Absolutely." The knowledge came from deep within, and filled him with wonder and pride. It was so all-encompassing, he felt as if his whole world had changed.

He rubbed his thumb over the back of Annie's hand. "Thank you. For giving me a son and for being patient with me when I screwed up."

She cleared her throat. "Micah is lucky to have a father like you."

The connection between them was strong, solid. Until Micah crawled between them, wiggling his rear end to fit.

Annie smiled and moved to accommodate him.

Drew met Annie's gaze over the top of Micah's head, and wished they were like this all the time.

Annie cleared her throat. "Um, Micah, you know how most of your friends have a daddy and a mommy?"

He nodded, his expression solemn, as if he knew this was a momentous conversation.

"Well, you have a daddy and a mommy, too," she continued. "I'm your mommy and Drew is your daddy."

Micah's eyes widened and he turned to gaze at Drew. "Daddy? *My* daddy?" he breathed.

"That's right, buddy." He waited for the boy's reaction.

He didn't have to wait long. Micah threw himself in Drew's arms and held on tight. "Daddy."

"Yes, I am. And I love you very much."

Though Annie smiled, she seemed subdued.

He touched her shoulder. "Hey, are you okay?"

She nodded, her eyes bright.

"You sure?"

"It's just that I never realized how much it meant to him. That at less than two years old he was feeling the void."

Micah clambered into her lap from Drew's, patting her cheek. "Daddy live here?"

"Oh, no, honey. It's going to be like Chase's family. Daddy will have his own apartment and he'll visit you here and sometimes you'll visit him there."

Micah nodded, but Drew could tell he couldn't wrap his mind around their situation. It was hard enough for an adult to figure out.

The boy settled close to Drew, apparently not needing any more explanation. Micah knew he could count on Drew and that was what was important.

"What time do we need to be at the barbecue?" Annie asked, her voice only slightly strained.

"I told Beth we'd be there about four o'clock."

"I better get those brownies on a plate then."
Annie stood and went to the kitchen.

An overwhelming sense of contentment stole over Drew as he listened to the ordinary noises in the kitchen and held his son on his lap.

This was a blessing he never could have imagined two years ago. It made him wonder what other phenomenal adventures were in store for them.

ANNIE BARELY LISTENED AS Micah chattered in his car seat. She was too busy anticipating meeting Drew's friends.

What would they be like? What would they think of Micah? Of her?

Then an awful thought struck her. "You didn't give Beth the details of how we…met, did you?"

"Not the intimate details, no."

"But she knows about the one-night—" she glanced over her shoulder and lowered her voice to a whisper "—stand?"

"I don't remember exactly what I told her. I was still stunned to think I had a son."

"So I didn't matter?"

"Of course you mattered. Where is this going?"

Annie pushed up her glasses. "I'm nervous, okay? What if she doesn't like me? What if she thinks I'm…a bad person?"

Drew laughed. "Oh, believe me, the only one she'll think was bad is me."

Annie rolled her eyes. "You're getting way too much enjoyment out of this."

"It's kind of a nice change of pace. I've been jumping through hoops trying to prove I could be a competent dad when I felt like the biggest loser of all time."

"You were just a little uninformed," she teased. "But you've made vast improvements."

"Thanks. I'm glad to hear that. Maybe it will be good for you to see me in my element."

That's what bothered her. She'd learned to like Drew within the narrow context of their relationship, such as it was.

What if she found out something she couldn't stand about him?

Annie let it go. Everything would be fine. It was, after all, only one afternoon.

She was surprised when they drove into a subdivision in Chandler of half-acre lots and custom homes. This area was on the upper end of middle class.

Several cars and trucks were parked in the circular drive and Drew had to search for a space to park along the street.

"It looks like quite a party."

"Yeah, Beth and Orion really know how to get

everyone together. But I think this is the first party I've been to here since Orion...was killed."

Annie opened her mouth to ask more about him, but Drew shut off the engine and Micah was struggling against his restraints.

So she got out and went around to the vehicle, but Drew had beat her to it.

He was unbuckling the harness, lifting Micah from his seat.

"Down," the boy demanded.

"Hold my hand," Drew countered as he set him on his feet, grasping his hand before Micah realized he had a choice.

She took her son's other hand and they headed up the walk.

The rye grass was lush and dark green, the orange trees neatly trimmed. It was obvious someone took great care of the landscaping. Did Beth try to do it herself? Was she one of those perfect, Martha Stewart–type women?

Annie's nervousness returned.

Drew didn't bother to knock on the door. He merely let them in.

There was music playing, and laughter drifted in through an open window.

"Usually everyone hangs out in the back-yard," he explained.

They went through a large country kitchen.

He nodded toward the center island. "Why not leave the brownies there if you can find a spot."

Annie wedged her plate among the array of cupcakes and cookies. The back counter held a casual buffet of plates, condiments, salads and deviled eggs.

Annie ran her hand over the cool, smooth surface. "Granite. I have counter envy."

Drew grinned. "Funny, I never would have figured you for a kitchen slu—" He stopped himself just in time. "Floozy."

She smacked him playfully on the arm. "Watch it, Vincent. The child repeats every new word he hears. Particularly the ones you don't want repeated."

"Yes, Beth warned me about that."

A beautiful African-American woman came into the room and extended her hand. "You must be Annie. I'm Beth. I've been looking forward to meeting you."

She enfolded Annie's hand in a soft, firm grip that was somehow reassuring.

The tension eased from Annie's shoulders. "Nice to meet you, Beth. What a lovely home."

"Annie was coveting your granite counter-tops," Drew told her.

"Floozy," Micah added.

Beth raised an eyebrow and laughed. She extended her hand to the boy. "And it's so wonderful to see you again, little man."

Micah reached up for Drew's hand. "Me daddy."

She glanced up at Drew, then Annie for confirmation. "Is he telling me what I think he's telling me?"

"Yep, I'm his dad." Drew's grin couldn't possibly get any bigger. "We told him earlier this afternoon."

Beth placed her palm on Micah's head, almost like a benediction. "You have a fine daddy, Micah. And I can see you are a fine son."

And what am I, the incubator? But Annie managed not to utter the thought aloud.

Beth turned to her. "Which of course is from having a dedicated mother. I'm a firm proponent of the theory that the hand that rocks the cradle rules the world."

Annie liked the woman. There was a quiet strength about her that seemed so peaceful.

"Thank you."

"Oh, I include myself in that. So you see, my theory isn't completely altruistic. Now, Micah, there are some children outside who are just dying to have you play with them."

Micah took her hand without hesitation, and Annie shook her head in surprise as she and Drew followed them through the sliding glass door to the patio.

CHAPTER FIFTEEN

IN BETH'S BACKYARD, Drew and Micah were instantly absorbed by the festive crowd.

Annie held back, once again feeling out of place.

She watched as the children drew her son off to a grassy area where they were having a game of Red Rover. He was placed on the end, holding Beth's granddaughter's hand. There seemed to be tacit agreement to play gently with Micah. None of the children tried to break through the line where his hand was linked with the girl's.

Micah laughed uproariously when a preteen boy finally pretended to do so, then seemed awed by Micah's great strength. The toddler, of course, loved every minute of it.

"He's a darling boy."

Annie turned to find a willowy brunette addressing her.

"Yes, he is."

"I'm Vanessa. Steve's my husband."

She indicated the big bruiser wrapping Drew in a bear hug. "He's glad to see Drew, can you tell?"

Annie laughed, "I'm Annie Marsh. And yes, I can tell."

"They've got some kind of superhuman bond. It comes from serving together in Iraq. Sometimes I feel left out. It's as if they speak a language I can't understand. But I'm glad he has friends like Drew. Now, while he's adjusting to being back. And when he was over there, too."

"I didn't know Drew then."

Vanessa glanced at Micah. "He's what, almost two? Seems as if you and Drew were at least passing acquaintances."

Annie's face grew warm. She'd never had to deal with innuendo when everyone thought Micah's father was dead.

"Of course I knew him. But, um, not well."

Vanessa's smile was warm. "No need to get embarrassed. I fell for Steve the first time I laid eyes on him. Boom. I was a goner. I can't wait till we have a little boy who looks just like him."

"You think Micah resembles Drew that much?"

"Absolutely. I would have known even if I hadn't overheard Drew crowing about it the minute he walked in."

Annie watched the byplay between the guys. The slaps on the back and elbow nudges made her angry. Drew should have asked her before he told everyone about his relationship to Micah.

Her anger slowly dissipated as she noticed Drew's joy. It was as if he'd won the lottery, flung the opening pitch at the D-backs game and been awarded the Nobel Peace Prize all in one day.

She would have cheated both of them horribly if she hadn't told Drew the truth about his son.

"You want to come sit with me and the other women? I think your boys are going to be occupied for a while."

"Yes, I'd like that. Thanks."

DREW FELT AS IF HE'D come home. And in a way he had.

He found Mac and got caught up on all the news from Iraq. Then he talked some trash to Steve as he passed the barbecue where his buddy pretended to be King of the Grill.

Searching the cluster of children, Drew spotted Micah riding on a teen's shoulders. Then he went and found Annie. Her expression was animated as she sat at a large round table shaded by an umbrella, chatting with Beth's oldest daughter, Ivy.

"So everything I've read is true? I don't need to worry because he isn't interested yet?" Annie asked.

"He's obviously a bright, healthy boy. The male of the species just can't keep up with us, even in potty training."

"Not fair," Drew protested.

"But true." Ivy raised an eyebrow when he rested his hand on Annie's shoulder.

"Hey, ladies, the great outdoor chef tells me the burgers are almost ready, so you might want to give the potty training a rest."

"Spoken like a true man...who hasn't changed a zillion diapers," Annie commented.

"Or gotten sticker shock buying them."

Though Ivy's comment was innocent, Drew shifted uncomfortably. He hadn't seriously considered Annie's expenses. He'd have to make arrangements to help out until they decided on a more formal agreement.

He squeezed her shoulder. "Annie, why don't you go ahead and get yourself something to eat before these hungry guys hog all the food. You, too, Ivy."

Annie stood, tucking her hair behind her ear. Drew liked it loose and flowing.

"I'll make a plate for Micah," she said. "He's probably too excited to eat much, but I've got to try."

"I'm right behind you," Ivy called, also standing.

"Don't let this one get away," she whispered to Drew as she passed by.

He pretended ignorance even though he knew exactly what she meant. Annie was…an enigma to him. He wasn't sure she'd be interested in him under normal circumstances. The night they'd met had been a lucky coincidence that couldn't have been recreated if they'd tried. Could it?

Annie returned and set down her plate, napkin and plastic cutlery on the table.

"Would you mind getting Micah? I'll put his food with the other children." She nodded toward one of the two kid-size picnic tables.

"Sure. If this is anything like the birthday party, he'd much rather sit with the kids than with us."

Drew went and found Micah still piggypacking on Steve's nephew Gabe. Drew hoped Annie didn't see that, for she'd probably come unglued.

Stepping close, he said, "Hey, buddy, time for food."

Micah folded his arms over his chest. "No."

"Come on, kid. Your mom's already got you a plateful."

"No!"

Drew got a hold of him under the arms, but Micah locked his legs around Gabe's neck.

"Come on."

Micah started to screech.

"I know you want to play, but it's time to eat. You can play more after you eat."

"No. Play now."

The teen's face reddened. Drew was afraid Micah might strangle the boy with his grip.

"You leave me no choice. I'll have to resort to drastic measures."

He tickled Micah under the arms until the child loosened his grip long enough for Drew to pull him off.

Micah kicked and screamed, enraged.

Drew felt as if every last person at the party was staring at him. Judging him. Figuring he was a failure as a dad because he couldn't control his son.

Tucking the writhing child under his arm like a football, he headed toward Annie.

She met him halfway, taking Micah from him. Then she laid the boy on the grass while he kicked and screamed out his frustration.

"Shouldn't we do something?"

210 WELCOME HOME, DADDY

"Nothing to do but let him work it out."

"There's got to be something more we can do."
He started to sweat. He caught Ivy staring at them.

She gave him a thumbs-up.

Annie gently shook her son's shoulders. "Micah, stop it."

And he did. For all of about five seconds.

"Micah, when you're ready to act like a big boy, come find Mommy and I'll show you where your food is. Now, I'm going to eat."

"You're just going to leave him here?"

She turned and casually walked toward their table, as if their son wasn't making this huge scene.

Drew glanced at Micah, who continued to screech, but then watched Annie intently.

Shrugging, Drew followed her. "Are you sure you know what you're doing?"

She stopped, turning to him. "Are you kidding? It goes against every instinct I have as a mother. But he's young and time-outs don't seem effective. My mom suggested this solution. It works."

"Is there…something wrong with him?"

"Absolutely not!" She scowled at Drew. "He's just a normal, overstimulated little boy starting the terrible twos."

"Okay, okay. No need to get upset. I'm just

trying to understand. Temper tantrums are new to me."

He could feel the fight go out of her.

Her chin quivered. "Every stage is like starting over again. And I'm so damn scared I'm going to do something wrong."

Stepping closer, he wrapped his arms around her, drawing her into a hug. He knew his friends were watching, but he didn't care. Annie needed him.

"It'll be okay. You're a terrific mom. So terrific that I know I can't measure up no matter how hard I try."

She sniffled for a moment before tilting her head back to meet his gaze. "Thanks, I needed a shoulder to cry on. I try not to let Micah see when it gets to me. And I really want your friends to like us."

Drew traced her cheek with his fingers. "They adore you. Now, let's eat before our food gets cold. Or Micah pulls something new out of his bag of tricks."

"Comforting him when he's sick or sad seems to come naturally for me. But tantrums are the worst."

"He's just learning to push buttons. Face it, it's probably effective with most adults. We give in to children just to get them to quit screaming."

Her smile wobbled a bit, but he sensed she was over the worst of it.

Conversation picked up again as they headed toward the table. Everyone seemed intent on pretending they hadn't witnessed anything out of the ordinary.

Everyone except Ivy. She winked and said, "I'd say Micah has his daddy's stubbornness."

That broke the tension and they all laughed. Conversation resumed in earnest and Drew felt as if he'd conquered some amazing challenge.

He felt someone pat his arm.

Looking down in his son's tearstained face, he felt his heart grow about six sizes—just like the Grinch. "Hey, buddy, I'm glad you decided to join us."

Micah rested his head against Drew's hip for a moment. Then wedged himself into Annie's lap.

"Are you tired, sweetie?" she murmured.

Micah didn't answer, simply slipped his thumb in his mouth and went boneless in her arms.

Ivy handed him a buttered hamburger bun. "He played pretty hard with the older kids. It probably tuckered him out trying to keep up. My youngest still throws a tantrum if she gets overtired. Mom's got the guest bedroom all childproofed. Let me know when you want him to nap, and I'll show you."

Micah chewed on the bun, his eyelids drooping. "No…nap," he mumbled.

Drew hoped they weren't in for a repeat performance. "Man, have I got a lot to learn."

Annie rested her hand on his arm. "We both do."

He felt that heart expansion thing happen again. Only this time, he was also afraid. How could he be so reckless as to fall for Annie? Their situation was complicated enough without muddying it up with some sort of chemical attraction.

Or worse yet, falling for her if she didn't feel the same….

ANNIE CONTINUED TO ROCK Micah for a few minutes even though he'd fallen asleep. Just to feel the weight of him in her lap, cuddled to her chest. To inhale the scent of his shampoo and try not to mourn the passing of his babyhood.

The quiet soothed her after an afternoon spent with a bunch of strangers. They were wonderful people, but she felt them watching. Measuring her worth as a mother and as a companion to Drew. Did they realize there was no romantic relationship?

But recalling the way Drew had stroked her cheek, she was sure he cared for her. Would that be a bad thing?

She rested her head against Micah's. She just didn't know. Drew's life was becoming enmeshed with theirs when she had naively thought they could keep it compartmentalized—neat and safe.

She had the feeling things could get a whole lot messier and she simply didn't know what to do to stop it.

Finally, when she couldn't hide any longer, Annie placed Micah on the bed, tucking pillows in on either side so he wouldn't roll off. She snagged a diet soda from the cooler on her way outside, sparing only one longing glance at Beth's kitchen.

The woman herself materialized when Annie walked outside. "Did you get him to sleep?"

"Yes. He was out like a light once he quit fighting it."

"Poor guy. Probably afraid he might miss something. Would you like to sit with me in the shade over there? Or would you rather join the volleyball game?"

Annie smiled as she eyed the raucous teams, which included adults, children and a golden retriever. "Today, I'm grateful to sit out."

They walked over and sat on two upholstered wicker chairs. Beth sighed, propping her feet on a matching ottoman. "Oh, this is what I needed. I've forgotten how wonderfully exhausting a group this size can be."

"Yet you make hosting seem so effortless."

"It's a joy. Especially having the soldiers here that Orion loved like sons. But...I miss my husband."

Annie's heart went out to the woman. "I'm so sorry for your loss."

Beth smiled. "Thank you. It helps having his friends and their children around. I'm so glad Drew was able to bring you and Micah today. I've never seen him happier."

Annie warmed at the compliment. "Really?"

"Fatherhood agrees with him. I think you do, too."

"We're not...dating or anything."

"That surprises me. Because he looks at you as if he wishes you were."

"Drew and I...didn't know each other well when Micah was conceived. So I'm learning about him as we go along." Annie was mortified that she'd confided the one fact she'd wanted to keep under wraps.

But Beth inspired confidence.

"What would you like to know about him?"

There was a mischievous glint in the woman's eyes. "His bad habits? Old girlfriends?"

"Wow. Carte blanche. And I can't think of a thing. I'm sure I'll remember a zillion questions after we leave."

"Then you'll have to call me. I can tell you that Drew is an extraordinary man. He has great heart and loyalty. And depth."

"I've noticed he seems to miss Orion."

Beth seemed absorbed in the volleyball game. "How much has he told you about his time in Iraq?"

"Drew said he feels really close to the people he served with. I get the feeling he still feels responsible for them, and maybe a little guilty that he came home while some are still there. And he told me about the day that…Orion died."

Nodding, Beth said, "Orion's death hit him particularly hard. They had a special bond. Closer almost than father and son. I don't think Drew has completely processed his grief. Could be he's afraid to let himself feel it."

"He hasn't confided in me much about his feelings. He said the army isn't good about getting them the kind of counseling they need. But that was mostly about what they could expect adjusting to being home again."

Beth shrugged. "The army does the best it can. But the sheer number of soldiers who need help is overwhelming. And many of the guys won't ask for it. Orion was the one Drew would have opened up to about something like this."

"What do you think he would tell Orion?"

"That he never should have died on that road to Mosul. That Drew would trade places with him if he could. And that he feels responsible when he really shouldn't."

"Drew feels responsible?"

"Yes." Beth eyes misted. "Orion died because he took Drew's seat. It was a joke and so like my husband...."

CHAPTER SIXTEEN

DREW WATCHED STEVE down another beer as if it were water. His friend didn't stagger, didn't slur his words, and that's what particularly concerned Drew. That and the fact that it was somehow disrespectful to get hammered at Beth's house during her first party since Orion's death. He'd never known Steve to be disrespectful to a woman or superior officer. And in a way, Beth was both.

Drew tried to tell himself it wasn't his business.

But something prodded him to follow Steve to the ice chest a few minutes later.

Steve was reaching for another beer when Drew said, "Hey, I haven't had a chance to catch up with you today, find out what's going on stateside."

"Things are great. Who wouldn't want to be home?" The man had an edge to his voice.

"It was hard for me at first," Drew said slowly. "Things were so different from Iraq. I'd gotten used to being always on guard. It took me a while to figure out I didn't have to do that at home."

"You were just able to turn it off?" Steve asked quietly. "Because I can't. If I'm in public, I start feeling like I'm gonna crawl out of my skin. People get too close, crowds are noisy. It's like there's an enemy I can't see, but I know he's there."

Drew nodded. "Yeah, I know what you mean." Although his own reaction hadn't been quite that severe, it wasn't uncommon.

He moved off to the side, inching toward a couple of lawn chairs in a corner. Quiet, enclosed spaces tended to be reassuring for someone with post-traumatic stress disorder. At least, that's what Orion had said.

Sitting, he motioned to the other chair.

Steve sat, but his foot jiggled nervously.

"Does the beer help?" Drew asked.

"It mellows me out so I can function."

"That's what I was afraid of. Orion always said needing a substance to function was a sign of a problem."

"I'm not an alcoholic. I drink a few beers to relax."

"But if you start to wonder if it's more, let someone know. They've got programs that can help."

"If you can get in," his friend muttered. "There are thousands of other guys having a hard time adjusting. It'll just take time." But it didn't sound as if he had much hope.

What scared Drew was Steve's smell of fear—a musky variation of body odor that he'd sometimes noticed before he went out on patrol. Usually after he'd had a close call. Or a buddy had been killed.

"Sometimes it takes more than time. Don't be too stubborn to ask for help."

"I can't, Drew." The words seemed torn from him. "Vanessa thinks things should be normal now that I'm home. She deserves the husband she had before I went over there."

Drew saw Annie walk outside, clearly searching for him. He wanted to gesture to her, but had to give Steve his complete attention.

"Nobody understands," Steve declared. "Except the guys who were there."

"Then those are the ones you ought to find. They probably need to talk about it as much as you do."

"Group therapy? No way."

"It doesn't have to be. I hear there are some good blogs and chat rooms online. Or if you can handle it, maybe just getting together with some guys to shoot pool and shoot the shit. Or bowl. Or play poker."

"You hear about some group like that, you let me know."

It was more of a challenge than an agreement to participate, but Drew was beginning to get an idea.

"I will," he finally said.

Steve jumped to his feet, his beer finished. "I better, um, go make sure the gas is shut off on the grill."

Drew figured they'd made progress when his friend got a soda out of the ice chest.

He sat there for a moment, thinking about what he wanted to do with the life God had given him. He'd avoided making a decision so far, but he doubted he'd be able to avoid it much longer.

Annie came over and sat in Steve's recently vacated chair. "That looked serious. I didn't want to interrupt."

Drew ran a hand through his hair. "Just trying to be there for a friend in need. Not sure how well I did."

"Sometimes it helps just to know someone cares enough to ask how you're doing, and actually listen when you tell them.

"I'm a man and men want to fix things. I

want to tell him he's got PTSD and needs treatment, or it will only get worse."

"Did you?"

"No, I didn't think he was ready to hear it. I'm afraid he'll have to hit bottom before he'll get help. And even if he does, I'm not sure what will be there for him. Maybe I can check into it for Vanessa."

"I bet she'd appreciate that. It's got to be tough for you, too, watching your friend go through something like that."

"Frustrating as hell. It shouldn't be that way. These guys shouldn't have to come home and feel lost. Like they don't belong anywhere."

Annie touched his cheek, her fingers tentative, but oh so welcome. "Maybe there's something else you can do?"

He clasped her hand and held it to his cheek for a moment. Kissing her palm, he twined his fingers in hers and lowered their hands to his knee.

"I *know* there's something else I can do. But you're not going to like it."

"Why would I object to you helping your friends?" She pulled her hand away. "Do you think I'm that insecure?"

"It's just that I feel I'm being led down a path that's going to make it difficult to be the…kind of family man I want to be." *Or you want me to be.*

"What are you talking about?"

"I want to rejoin the army and become a chaplain, so I can be there with these guys when they need someone the most, before they ship home." The certainty expanded till there was no more room for doubt. "And that means deployment."

The color drained from Annie's face. She stood. Though she stared down at him, her gaze went over his left shoulder, as if she didn't really see him. As if she'd already made up her mind.

"I can't talk about this right now." She gestured toward the crowd in the yard. "Especially not here."

"Annie, I—"

She turned and walked away.

Drew had never felt more alone.

ANNIE ATE HER LUNCH in the teachers' lounge, making room for Kara Barton. The sign language translators were essentially in social no-man's-land. They weren't teachers, though most teachers welcomed their presence. And they weren't aides, either. It took special training and accreditation to be an interpreter.

"Hi, Annie," Kara said, tucking her silvery-blond hair behind her ear. With her tiny frame and pert nose, she could almost have passed for one of the students.

"Hi."

"How's your day going?"

Annie cleared her throat, wishing she and Kara had a close friendship. She needed someone now. But something held her back from confiding. "Okay. Wish I didn't have to stay late today, though. I have so many things to do at home. I don't think Micah has a set of clean clothes left."

"Want me to take your practice?"

Annie considered it for a nanosecond. The pay was good and she needed the extra cash. But ultimately, she couldn't face the loss she'd feel if she didn't see Drew during the week. She needed him to keep babysitting.

"Thanks, but I need the money. You'll be the first one I call if I have a scheduling conflict, though."

"Please do."

Annie unwrapped her sandwich. She'd be glad when Micah outgrew his penchant for peanut butter and jelly. He'd been particularly enthralled when he'd seen the commercial for peanut butter and jelly combined in one jar. It didn't get any better than that for a two-year-old. And unfortunately, she hadn't had time to shop for the lunch meat she preferred.

"So tell me about Drew." The predatory gleam in the woman's eyes put Annie on alert. Kara acted like a woman on the trail of a juicy story.

"He's a friend."

"Oh." Her disappointment was evident. "Because I volunteered yesterday at the preschool and Micah said something interesting during show and share time."

Annie suppressed a groan. Show and share was every parent's nightmare, because eventually a child was bound to reveal something so personal, so mortifying, that the parent was never able to look the teacher in the eye again. Her friend Marlene, who taught kindergarten, had confirmed the fact.

A bite of sandwich lodged in Annie's throat. Sipping her soda, she managed to wash it down. "Oh?"

"He said he had a daddy."

"Well, of course. Everyone has a father."

"He said his daddy's name was Drew."

Crud. If she confirmed it to Kara, the whole school would know. Gossip traveled faster than the speed of light around this place.

Sighing, she faced the music. "Drew *is*

Micah's father. It's a long and complicated story and I really don't want to go into the details."

"Are you going to get married?" Kara breathed, as if Annie's life was the stuff of romantic fairy tales.

"We're just friends."

"I doubt that. He sure looked like he wanted to be more than friends."

"It's not going to happen, Kara. He's a good guy, he'll make a terrific father for Micah…"

No matter how noble his reason, Drew was intent on putting himself in danger right along with his friends, and that meant hands off.

"…but he's just not for me." A hollow ache took Annie by surprise.

"That's too bad." Kara's smile faded. "I so wanted someone to be having wild monkey sex. And it certainly isn't me."

The improbability of hearing the term "wild monkey sex" coming out of Kara's decidedly Waspish mouth distracted Annie from her misery. And made her view her colleague more kindly.

"Bob's not, um, rocking the bedroom, huh?"

"No, most of the time he sleeps on the sofa in his den." Kara's expression was so forlorn that Annie forgave her for participating in her husband's snide remarks about single mothers.

"That's too bad."

"I suppose it's just a normal part of married life. I mean, it can't always be fireworks, can it?"

It was a relief to focus on Kara's problem and avoid her own. "If it's bothering you, talk to him."

"I have. He just changes the subject. I'm worried that he's…having an affair."

"Maybe counseling?"

"I was hoping since you're single and uh, hip, you might know of some ways I could spice things up. Get him interested again."

Annie coughed, glad she'd taken only a small sip of soda. Otherwise it might be squirting out her nose. "I don't lead nearly as exciting a life as you might think. But I've seen ads for stores that sell…toys. Maybe do some shopping?"

Too bad Kat wasn't here. She could probably give personal recommendations. But Annie hadn't so much as looked at a vibrator even with her nonexistent love life.

"I'll do that. Thanks." Kara smiled in relief, as if all it would take was a new toy to turn Bob into a tiger.

Annie glanced at her watch. She squeezed Kara's arm and stood. "I've got to run. I'm sure things will work out."

DREW WAS NORMALLY EAGER for Annie to get home, but not today. It had been three days since Beth's party and Annie would not discuss his career plans. He'd stopped by on Sunday, but she'd refused to let him in, saying he needed to call first. When he called on Monday, her phone went straight to voice mail.

It looked an awful lot like she was trying to shut him out of her life, while allowing him the bare minimum contact with Micah.

Drew surveyed the chaos of the great room and went over to turn off the TV. "Hey, buddy, better clean up your toys. Your mom will be home soon."

"No."

Drew grabbed Micah and tossed him in the air. "Did I hear you say no?"

The boy giggled.

"When does the 'yes' stage start?" He tossed him again.

Micah laughed.

Drew set him on the ground.

"Wrestle!"

"If I wrestle with you, will you pick up your toys?"

"Yes!"

"Finally, a yes." Drew wrestled him to the

floor, tickling him until he couldn't tell where one giggle left off and the next began.

He stopped to let Micah catch his breath.

A few seconds later, the boy flung himself at Drew as he knelt to pick up train parts, causing him to topple backward.

Micah climbed on his chest and bounced in victory. "Me won!"

"Oh, you're killing me," Drew groaned.

He bounced harder, then jumped up and did a body slam. Drew wheezed as he tried to regain his breath.

Micah didn't seem fazed. Maybe it was the adrenaline rush he had going. The kid leaped up, prepared to do it again.

"No!" Drew shielded himself with his arms.

Micah started at him with windmill punches.

"Oh, man, cut it out. That's the last time I let you watch WWF with me. No soda, either."

"That should have been a no-brainer," a female voice said from behind him.

Drew hoped like crazy Kat had dropped in for an unscheduled visit. But he knew better.

"Annie?" he wheezed.

"None other."

"Did I get another demerit as a father?"

"Demerits are the least of your worries."

CHAPTER SEVENTEEN

STANDING THERE IN THE great room, angry as hell, Annie only wished her irritation was because of Drew's roughhousing with Micah.

No, it was the crushing realization that Drew was merely a short-lived blip on their radar screen.

He let out an "oof" as Micah got in one last slam.

"Micah James. That's enough." Her mom tone stopped him in his tracks.

Drew groaned as he struggled to his feet. "You're going to have to teach me that trick."

She crossed her arms. "You'll develop your own technique. Besides, you won't be needing it much, being out of the country. I'll be the one dealing with the aftershocks."

"Annie, it doesn't have to be this way."

"Doesn't it? I didn't get the impression there was much room for compromise. You've decided what you want. If I needed proof of how little we mean to you, that was it."

Drew frowned and stepped closer. "That's not it at all." He reached for her.

She held up her hand. "Don't."

"I should have waited until I had it all sorted out in my mind. I handled the conversation badly and I'm sorry."

"So it would have been better that I had no idea? If I continued to grow to depend on you and…care…when there's really no future for us?"

"Mommy mad?" Micah tugged on her pant leg.

She picked him up, holding him tight, reminding herself that they'd been just fine before Drew had shown up.

Closing her eyes, she rested her forehead against Micah. "No, sweetie, I'm just…disappointed."

He wrapped his arms around her neck and patted her back, just as she did when he was upset. It brought a lump to her throat and made her feel even more vulnerable.

"Annie, could Kat take Micah for a while, do you think?"

She opened her eyes and wished she hadn't. Drew looked so strong and solid standing there, as if he could be an immovable support in their lives.

But she knew how fleeting life was once a strong man made up his mind to pursue danger. Her father had seemed superhuman until she'd seen his body crumpled at the base of a mountain.

"I don't know," she murmured. "I just don't know."

"You said I wasn't willing to compromise, but you didn't give me a chance to try. You just walked off, and barely spoke to me on the way home from Beth's."

"What's to explain, Drew? You've made your choice and you made the situation very clear. We're just a diversion to you."

"You know that's not true." He squared his shoulders. "I love Micah. And I've got… feelings…for you."

Annie was dismayed by how badly she wanted to believe him, how badly she wanted to walk into his arms. "Enough to make a difference in your plans?"

Desperation flashed in his eyes. "Enough that I'm willing to look into staying stateside. Or places that aren't combat zones, but are close to the guys in need or injured, like Germany. Who knows, maybe you and Micah could come with me."

Annie's breath caught in her throat. "What are you saying? This is happening too fast."

Micah squirmed. "Down."

Drew took him from her and set him on his feet. Swatting him lightly on the rump, he said, "Go play with your trucks while your mom and I talk."

He cupped her face with his hand, kissing her, just a light touch of the lips, but enough to remind her how much they'd once shared. "Drew, I—"

"Shh. Hear me out. This is all new. Let's drop back a few paces and give ourselves room to explore this. We deserve to know if we could be a family someday."

Annie leaned against him, wanting what he described so badly and wondering why she hadn't seen it before. Day by day, little by little, she'd been falling for him.

She let her gaze rove over his face, searching for hidden motives. There were none. Just a wonderful, strong, giving man who wanted a chance.

Though it scared her, Annie knew she had to give him that chance. To give the three of them that chance.

"Okay," she whispered. "We'll see where it leads."

"You won't be sorry," he promised, his voice husky. Dipping his head, he kissed her again, really kissed her.

Annie relaxed into him, murmuring his name as he deepened the kiss. And she knew she was home.

DREW WAS RELUCTANT TO turn Annie loose. Kissing her took him back to that wonderful, crazy evening Micah had been conceived, but this was so much better now that he knew the real Annie.

Aware of Micah playing trucks by the coffee table, he reluctantly relinquished her, gratified that her cheeks were flushed and she seemed disoriented.

"Spend the weekend with me? Both of you?" The question was out before he could censor it. "I mean, I could sleep here on your couch…."

Annie glanced away. "Even on the couch, it might confuse Micah."

"Micah or you?"

She hesitated. "Both."

"Just think about it?"

"You don't know how tempting it is." She stepped back a pace and he could almost feel her pulling back emotionally, too. "But no, we can't."

"Let's at least spend Saturday together. All of us."

"Well, I guess…."

His hopes rose.

Shaking her head, she said, "I'm sorry, Drew, I forgot. We're going up to my mom's cabin in Payson this weekend."

"That means I won't see you at all."

Micah tugged on Annie's pant leg. "Daddy come Granmma's?"

"Um, I don't think so, sweetie."

"You've got to admit, it's a good solution. I'd get to meet your mom and Micah's grandmother, and you and I would be properly chaperoned. Both you *and* your mother would be there to give me child-rearing pointers."

Annie tapped her chin.

"Please?" Micah was at his most persuasive.

Annie smiled. "You two don't play fair. I'll call Grandma tonight and see if it's okay with her."

Micah wrapped his arms around her thigh and hugged for all he was worth. "Yay!"

"We don't know for sure Grandma will say yes…."

But Micah didn't seem to hear her. To him, it was a done deal.

Drew only hoped that Micah had his grandmother wrapped as tightly around his finger as Annie said.

DREW WHISTLED IN TUNE with the stereo as they headed up the Beeline Highway on Saturday morning. With Annie beside him and Micah in his safety seat in the back, everything seemed perfect, except for the small, nagging doubt that he might not be able to deliver on his promise to her. Would the army allow him to pick and choose his assignments? Would compromising to stay out of danger be a form of turning his back on the soldiers he felt compelled to help?

Drew resolved to put his doubts out of his mind. He was doing what he needed to do for his family, and it would all work out. For now, he needed to show Annie what a great father he could be. And how great they could be together as a couple, too. After this weekend, he'd bet she'd be sure.

"What are you grinning about?"

He glanced sideways at her. "Nothing in particular. It just seems like a beautiful day for a drive."

"You certain you don't mind driving? We could have taken my car."

"We've got more cargo room in the truck. And with all the stuff you brought for Micah, we need it. You really think we'll use all this?"

"You still have to ask?"

He chuckled. "No, I guess not. Micah seems

a little big to be sleeping in the portable play-pen, though."

"I know. But I haven't figured out an alternative yet. He'll fall out if he sleeps in Mom's bed. And I don't want him running around unsupervised in the loft while we're sleeping. I'm afraid he'll take a tumble."

Drew patted Annie's knee, a friendly gesture. That is, until he imagined trailing his hand up her bare thigh.

Would a chaperone be able to keep his libido in line? His body was reminding him it had been a *very* long time.

He steered his thoughts toward the least sexy topic he could. "So, um, tell me about your mother."

A little recon before meeting her couldn't hurt, either.

"She's great. Strong and calm, with a bit of a free spirit thrown in. But she wasn't always so pulled together. It was rough after my dad died. It almost seemed as if she…died, too."

"How old were you?"

"Five."

He clasped her hand. "That's hard. I can't imagine… How did he die?"

Annie stared out the window. "A rock-climbing accident. It was awful."

"Losing a parent at that age would be hard for anyone, I'm sure."

"No, I mean the accident was awful. I saw him fall. I saw…his body land in the ravine."

Drew touched her hair, wishing he could hold her. "I'm so sorry," he murmured.

"I've always sworn my child would never have to face something like that. That's why I can't stand the thought of you being in combat. Being separated would be difficult, but knowing you were in danger every day would be impossible."

Drew's optimism plummeted. Could he honestly promise her he would never, *ever* be in a dangerous situation?

He could make that promise if he didn't rejoin the army. But he didn't think he could look himself in the mirror if he didn't. He released a frustrated sigh. The timing of it all just sucked.

"Hey, is something the matter?" Annie asked.

"Nah." He forced a smile, determined to enjoy this weekend. No decisions had to be made this very minute. "I, um, thought of a bill I forgot to pay before I left. So…we used to sing songs when we went on long car rides when I was a kid. Does Micah know any?"

"It just so happens—" Annie unzipped her

purse and pulled out a CD "—I brought something we could sing along to. The soundtrack to the *Veggie Tales* movie you bought him."

"Am I going to regret this?"

"No, it's not as bad as some. And Micah loves the songs."

"In that case, go ahead and pop it in." He tried hard to recover his former good mood. Mostly he succeeded.

Mostly.

ANNIE GREW NERVOUS AS they pulled into the circular drive outside the little A-frame.

As usual, her mother was out front watering. Except this time, June hesitated beside the unfamiliar truck. She didn't pounce on her grandson.

What if this weekend turned out to be a disaster? What if her mother didn't like Drew? She'd rarely liked the guys Annie had dated. But then again, in hindsight, none of them had been all that likable.

But Drew was a great guy through and through.

The thought made Annie sweat. She was afraid she was falling hard for the man.

"I'll get the squirt," Drew said as he shut off the engine and opened the door.

Annie got out and hugged her mom. "This is the first time you've ever come to greet me first."

June laughed. "It had absolutely nothing to do with the fact that I couldn't see through the tinted windows to check where Micah was."

Drew walked around the back of the truck, carrying a sleepy toddler.

"Hi, Mrs. Marsh. I'm Drew Vincent." He extended his hand.

"Call me June." She batted his hand away and gave him a hug that included Micah.

Annie was stunned. And somewhat irritated. She swung the diaper bag over her shoulder.

"You've never accepted any of the guys I've brought around. You've never been shy about letting them know, either. But all Drew has to do is get me knocked up and he's okay?"

"Annie, watch what you say. Little pitchers have—"

"Big ears." Micah clapped his hands.

Her mother beamed, as if Micah was the most gifted child on the planet. Which, of course, he was.

"Come here, you little dumpling." June extended her arms to him and he gladly transferred.

Drew fell into step with Annie. "I can see how easily replaced I am. I'll come out for the bags in a minute."

"Oh, Grandma is the supreme ruler of the

universe as far as he's concerned. They have kind of a mutual-admiration thing going on."

Drew gave her a funny look.

"What?" Annie asked.

"I have the feeling my mom will want a shot at that ruler of the universe title."

"I guess it would be unreasonable if I suggested you didn't tell her?"

"Yes." He hesitated. "It's tempting, though— my mom can be intense. That's why I put off telling her till we get back on Sunday."

Annie shrugged philosophically. "That's two days away. You may run screaming from here after a mere twenty-four hours with us. We're a scary bunch."

"Somehow I doubt that." He nudged her with his shoulder. "I like the Marshes. *All* of them." He whistled a tune as they climbed the steps to the A-frame.

CHAPTER EIGHTEEN

ANNIE DRIED THE LUNCH dishes after her mom washed and rinsed them. The familiar routine relaxed her. She savored the constants.

Especially since her relationship with Drew was so new and her emotions so intense.

"They're all just big kids, you know." Her mom gazed out the kitchen window to where Drew was showing Micah how to pitch horseshoes—Micah's were lightweight plastic in bright primary colors, Drew's were the real deal.

Micah picked up the horseshoe with both hands, squatted and did a granny shot.

"Men?"

"Yes. Look at the fun they're having."

"Everything can't be fun. It's a parent's job to teach a child."

"Definitely. But who says it can't be fun, too?"

"Mmm." Annie was afraid to embrace the once-familiar concept of fun. She wasn't sure she even remembered how, she'd been responsible for so long.

Placing the dry plate on the counter, she took another from the drainer, wondering what her life would have been like if her father had been a little less concerned with having fun and a lot more concerned with safety.

Yet as she watched Drew help Micah, holding his hands steady while he threw, she ached at the sight of them together, so in tune with each other.

"See, he's teaching him how to follow through." June's tone said "I told you so." "Follow through is important in life, as well as in sports."

"Yes, but it can be learned in other ways. I doubt there are many chess injuries in the emergency room. He actually allowed Micah to watch wrestling on TV the other day."

"Bumps and bruises are a part of growing up. And our children don't always take our preferences into account."

Annie glanced sideways at her mother. "Is there a point to that remark?"

"Several."

The twinkle in her mom's eyes made Annie smile. She nudged her with her shoulder. "Maybe I wouldn't make so many mistakes if you'd just come out and tell me what I'm doing wrong."

"Ah, but where's the lesson in that? The best lessons are those we learn for ourselves. I'll admit it's hard to watch your child get hurt in the process, though."

"But I know you're always there for me," Annie answered. "It gives me the courage to keep trying."

"And that's what you'll do for Micah."

Annie wasn't ready to cede the point. "What lessons have you learned for yourself?"

Her mom gazed out at the yard as if seeing something on the horizon. "I've learned that *never* can be a very long time."

"That's cryptic. Want to elaborate?"

June shook her head, her smile secretive.

"Why won't you tell me?" Then Annie noticed the heightened color in her mother's cheeks. "You've met someone, haven't you?"

When June didn't respond, she squealed, "You have! Who is he? How did you meet? Are you in love?"

"Shh. I'm not ready to share yet. It's still very new and I want to savor it."

Annie understood better than her mother probably knew. Wasn't that exactly how she felt about this fragile relationship starting with Drew? Still, the suspense was killing her.

"*Mom.* I hate secrets."

"I know you do, dear. But please, be patient."

"Patience is *not* one of my virtues, especially where secrets are concerned."

"Oh, I know. I will tell you one thing, though. He reminds me of your father. His spirit is very similar."

"Like Dad? Is he a daredevil?"

"Not a daredevil. But he relishes a challenge. He says that's what attracted him to me... He also reminds me a bit of your Drew."

Annie glanced away, unable to meet her mother's questioning gaze. "He's not *my* Drew."

Yet.

"If this mystery man's spirit is similar to Dad's, and Drew reminds you of the mystery man, does that mean Drew reminds you of Dad?"

"There are...similarities in their personalities."

Annie's stomach dropped. She studied Drew through the window. He was vital and strong, a man who would take care of himself and his loved ones. Hadn't he already proved that to her by compromising on his career choices?

As if sensing her scrutiny, Drew turned and waved—just as Micah picked up one of the iron horseshoes with both hands and whirled with it, colliding with the back of Drew's knees.

He let out a yelp and toppled.

Annie dropped the dish towel and ran outside. She reached Drew just as he was getting up.

Micah's eyes widened as he realized he'd hurt him. "Daddy?" He tentatively patted his leg.

"I'm okay, buddy. We need you to stick to the toy horseshoes a while longer. You're a strong kid!"

From the doorway June chuckled. "Yes, very similar."

Annie didn't know whether to scold Drew or Micah. So she simply turned and followed her mother into the house.

DREW ROCKED SLOWLY ON the porch swing, breathing deeply. The screened-in area allowed them to enjoy the chilly, pine-scented evening air without worrying about mosquitos.

Micah snuggled closer as Drew wrapped his arm around the boy. He felt such contentment he never wanted the moment to end.

Crickets chirped, and somewhere in the distance a coyote yipped.

The screen door squeaked and Annie's mother came out and settled in an Adirondack chair.

"You've got a beautiful place here, June."

"Thank you." She leaned her head back. "It suits me."

The swing creaked as Drew pushed with his foot.

"You care about my daughter." It wasn't a question.

"Yes, I do."

June's gaze was intense. "Do you love her?"

"You don't waste any time, do you?"

"No, I learned long ago that life's too fleeting to beat around the bush."

"I'm not sure how to answer your question."

"That's an answer in itself."

Drew could sense her disappointment. He couldn't put into words his feelings for Annie. But maybe he could set June's mind at ease.

"I would never knowingly hurt your daughter."

She smiled slightly. "That's good to know."

He rocked, she took a sip of her coffee.

As Micah started to nod off Drew placed a kiss on top of his head. "Big day, huh?"

Micah's only answer was to crawl into his lap. Drew cradled his son as the boy fell asleep.

"You're good for them." June's comment

took him by surprise. He'd almost forgotten she was there.

"I hope so. They're very good for me."

"Then we won't worry about the rest."

The screen door squeaked again as Annie came outside.

"Am I interrupting something?"

"No, we were just chatting, dear. Have a seat." June gestured to the spot on the swing Micah had vacated.

Drew slowed the swing with his foot, and after a moment's hesitation, Annie eased down next to him.

He started it in motion again.

She settled in, hip to hip with him, brushing back Micah's hair. "He's all tuckered out."

June got up. "Why don't I put him in his pajamas and tuck him into bed? I bet he won't even wake up."

"That would be nice, Mom. Thanks."

June lifted Micah from Drew's lap, murmuring, "Come on, sweetie. Grandma's got you."

Quiet descended after she went inside. Then the crickets tuned up again.

Annie sighed. "I love it here. It's so peaceful."

"Yeah. And the company's not bad, either. I like your mom."

"She likes you, too. Says you remind her of my dad."

Drew was pleased with the comparison. "And he was her great love."

"He *was* larger than life. I remember they used to laugh a lot. And touch. Even as a small child, I noticed that physical connection."

Drew stretched his arm out on the seat back behind her.

Annie rested her head on his arm. "My childhood before my dad died seems almost like a fairy tale to me now. We were so happy."

"How did you end up being there when the…accident happened?"

"We'd all gone on a picnic. Dad decided to take a short climb while my mom and I picked berries. I could see him moving up the face of the cliff. He reminded me of Spider-Man. I thought he was superhuman, that nothing bad could ever happen to him. And nothing bad could happen to us while we were with him."

Drew squeezed her shoulder. He wanted to spare her pain, wanted to be the one to protect her. But he wanted to know everything about her, the happy *and* the sad.

"What exactly happened?"

"He just fell. A freak thing. Nobody ever

figured out for sure why. I expected him to stand up and be okay. But he didn't."

"Wow."

"My whole life changed after that. It was like the bottom dropped out."

"I'm sorry, Annie."

She shrugged. "I got past it."

He had to wonder if she really *had* gotten past it. Wondered if she avoided risks because of the loss, not allowing Micah to enjoy regular boy stuff.

In the long run, did the reason matter? Understanding Annie's obsession wouldn't change her, and he wasn't sure he wanted to. Her vulnerability, as well as her strength, had been what attracted him the first night they'd met.

But as Micah's father, he would see that the boy had enough freedom to grow up like any other kid. He would pick his battles very carefully, though.

ANNIE GLANCED AROUND, enjoying the crystal-blue sky, the cool fresh breeze. The sight of Micah riding in a toddler backpack on Drew's shoulders. The knowledge that her mother was following them. It was a wonderful day to hike to the Water Wheel Falls.

By the time they reached the picnic area, the

straps of her small day pack were cutting into her shoulders. Yet Drew's stride never faltered as he carried Micah with ease.

Her mom caught up with her at a wide spot in the trail. "Your dad used to carry you like that."

"I've got vague memories…"

"You used to love riding in the pack. Or on his shoulders. You said you were a giant."

Annie suddenly remembered being way up high, laughing, as her father took huge steps. "He used to say 'Fee-fi-fo-fum.'"

"You do remember. I'm glad. You two were such great buddies."

"I couldn't have been much older than Micah. I just get flashes every now and then."

"He loved you very much, sweetheart. And he never would have voluntarily left us."

"Then why did he climb? He had to know it was dangerous." Annie's chest grew tight, though she didn't know if it was from emotion or the challenge of hiking and talking at the same time.

"He was always so sure of himself. He never perceived it as a danger."

"Well, he should have."

"I'm sorry his death left such a void. I know he wouldn't have wanted it that way. He would want you to be happy."

"My life is just fine."

But even as she said the words, Annie suspected that her mother was right. And she wondered what she might have been like had her childhood been carefree and safe, with both a loving father and a mother untouched by grief.

Sadness washed over her as she released a little of the hurt, the anger. The past was done. But she could try to make sure Micah's experience was better. He would never be turned upside down by loss.

Drew paused and waited for them to catch up. His grin made Annie almost weak in the knees.

Which made her wonder how she had possibly gotten to this point.

As if sensing her mood, Drew and Micah both set about cheering her up. And June was their willing accomplice.

Several hours later as she and Drew headed toward Phoenix on Highway 87, Annie sighed with contentment. "This was the best weekend I've had in a long time. Too long."

He squeezed her hand. "Same here," he said quietly. "It was everything I'd hoped."

For her, it was everything she hadn't dared to hope for in years.

CHAPTER NINETEEN

ANNIE WAS DISTURBED when they arrived at her place at dusk.

She didn't want Drew to leave.

He had removed Micah out of his seat and carried him through the door. The active weekend combined with the long drive made for a very sleepy boy.

"Go ahead to his room. I'll get him into some jammies and put him to bed."

Drew raised an eyebrow. "It's too early for bed, isn't it? Won't he be awake again later?"

Annie remembered giving Drew and Kat hell about letting Micah fall asleep around this time one evening. It would take a while for Drew to discover all the nuances to Micah's routine.

"He's so exhausted, I expect him to sleep through till tomorrow morning. He does that every once in a while after he's spent the weekend in Payson."

"Okay."

She followed them into Micah's room, bemused at how right it seemed to have Drew there. And again, how nice it was to have someone to share in the child-rearing duties. A bonus she'd never anticipated.

"You mind if I do this?" Drew asked.

"Not at all. I'll get out some clean pajamas."

After Micah was changed, Drew placed him in his crib and covered him with a lightweight blanket. Little did he know that Micah would kick his covers to the side long before morning.

Drew followed her out of the room.

She glanced over her shoulder at him and smiled. "Why are we tiptoeing? An earthquake wouldn't wake that child."

"Some sort of latent parental instinct?"

He hesitated in the family room. "I'll carry that stuff in and then be on my way."

"Would you like to stay for a bit? A glass of wine? Or cake and coffee?"

"I'm still full from that early dinner your mom made. But I'd like to stay for a few minutes."

"Okay. I can help—"

"No, you stay here with Micah."

He was back almost before she knew it, and there was a moment of awkwardness.

"Water or coffee?" she asked, busying herself in the kitchen.

"Water's fine."

When she returned with their drinks, she was glad to see he'd kicked off his shoes and was sitting on the couch as if he'd been around for years.

She sat next to him, close enough that she could absorb his warmth, get a whiff of his scent. Annie couldn't help but notice how great he looked in a snug, well-worn black T-shirt. He'd been in good shape before Iraq, but now he was all muscle.

Sipping her wine, she tried to get a handle on her emotions.

"Thanks again for taking me this weekend," he said.

"No thanks necessary. It was fun having you there."

"I enjoyed it even more than I expected. Sometimes I have to pinch myself to make sure this isn't all a dream. That Micah really is my son."

His admission made her eyes mist. "You're a terrific father," she admitted slowly.

"It means a lot to hear you say that." He brushed the hair from her face. "You're an amazing woman, Annie Marsh."

His simple statement touched her. "I think you're pretty amazing, too."

He cupped her chin with his hand and kissed her. "Would you go out with me on a real date?"

Annie allowed herself to study Drew without pulling back. To take in his stubbled jaw, tousled hair, brown eyes. Those same warm eyes she'd almost lost herself in the first evening they'd met.

"I'd like that."

It seemed as if her answer hung in the air.

"Good." Drew kissed the corner of her mouth, pulling her close and trailing kisses down her neck.

Annie angled her body to get nearer, seeking his mouth with hers.

It was all the encouragement he needed. Groaning, he parted her lips and kissed her with a passion reminiscent of their one night together. Only this time, Annie was sober, and her heightened senses told her how much she'd missed by being inebriated the first time.

Unbuttoning his flannel shirt, she ran her palms over the hard muscles of his chest, marveling at how good it felt to be with him. It went beyond his toned body and thrilling kisses. She'd seen Drew's wonderful soul revealed in the way he treated her and Micah, and loved every bit of him. Whatever the reason, she lost herself in the sensations of learning Drew.

And he seemed to want to learn every inch of her body, sliding his hands beneath her shirt and bra to cup her breasts. His breathing was harsh in her ear, every bit as rapid as hers.

"Let's—" She only got one word out before he kissed her again, a deep, possessive kiss.

Focus.

She had a child to consider. She broke off the kiss long enough to say, "My…room."

Drew groaned, leaning his head against the back of the couch.

When she started to rise, he grabbed her by the wrist and tugged her down again. Not on top of him, but next to him.

"We can't."

"Micah won't wake up. He's out for the night."

"I mean it's not…right."

Annie felt as if he'd struck her. How could he feel it wasn't right, when it was the most right thing she'd experienced in a long, long time?

He pulled her close and stroked her hair. Though it wasn't the kind of sexual intimacy she'd had in mind, it was precious nonetheless. She lay against his shoulder. "Help me understand."

"I had these intense, erotic dreams about Grace while I was in Iraq. Then I came back here and met Annie, and wanted you even more. The whole person, not just the fantasy woman dressed in Kat's clothes."

"And the problem is?"

"I want more for myself, more for you, than making love without a commitment. You said yourself it's not right to rush into things."

Annie knew she felt more for Drew than she'd ever felt for the men she'd slept with in her early college days. "What are you saying?"

"I made a promise to myself over there. Maybe I was just bargaining with God. 'If you let me live, I'll be a better man.' But I think it's more than that. It may sound old-fashioned, but I don't want to dishonor you. Yes, I had some intense dreams about you over there, but I also felt guilty about how I treated you. When we make love, I want to make sure we're both committed heart and soul."

The desire drained from her, replaced by an aching longing. She stroked his stubbled jaw, enjoying even this most innocent touch. "How can I argue with such a beautiful sentiment? Even if my body's telling me it's been way too long."

"Annie, I want you so bad it hurts. Literally. And it would be so easy to follow you to your room and spend the rest of the night having mind-blowing sex." He winced. "But in the morning, I'd see your beautiful face and know I owed you so much more. And I'd see Micah at the breakfast table and know I'd failed to set an example of what it means to be a man of honor."

Annie blinked away tears. "I don't think I've ever been rejected quite so beautifully before."

Drew groaned, wrapping an arm around her and drawing her close. He kissed her softly, lovingly, but without the heat she longed for. "I'm not even close to rejecting you. Just slowing it way down with the physical stuff."

The strong thud of his heart beneath her ear comforted her. Suddenly, it didn't matter as much that they hadn't made love. The sense of loss was still there, but she suspected he was promising her more.

"Then this is a good thing?"

"In the grand scheme, it's very good. It gives us a chance for our feelings to grow. And I can look you and Micah in the eye tomorrow, not to mention myself in the mirror. Besides, it keeps me right with God. How can that not be a good thing?"

Annie inhaled his musky, masculine scent, felt his chest ripple beneath her cheek as he smoothed the hair at her temple. If he'd been wonderful in bed when they were strangers, she had the feeling the Drew who cared about her would be phenomenal.

"Then it will be worth the wait," she murmured, ignoring her fear that she might commit to him only to lose him permanently.

CHAPTER TWENTY

DREW OPENED HIS MAILBOX and pulled out a manila envelope. The return address was that of the lab they'd used for the paternity test.

He grabbed a few bills from the back of the box, shut it and locked it.

His steps were surprisingly controlled as he took the cobbled path toward his apartment. Normally, he enjoyed the trip through the landscaped grounds, but today his thoughts were on the contents of the envelope.

He was so certain Micah was his son, the DNA results were just a formality.

When he reached his apartment, he set the mail on the coffee table and sliced open the large envelope with his pocket knife. His hands were steady as he took out the cover sheet and read the results.

Drew whooped with joy.

Micah was his son!

Son of his heart, son of his blood.

He picked up the phone and dialed. There was one person he most wanted to share the news with. One person who would appreciate what this meant to him.

"Hello."

"Annie, it's me. Drew. I got the lab results."

"Are they what you expected?"

"Absolutely. But there was just something about seeing it in black and white. I hope you understand...."

"I tried to put myself in your place and I realized how hard it must be for a guy. Women don't have to deal with that uncertainty, thank goodness."

Her understanding made him want to be with her all the more. She'd become an important part of his life in such a short time.

"I thought about you a lot today," he said.

"Good, because I thought about you, too."

"Any chance you and Micah would like to go for pizza to celebrate?"

"Hmm, pizza and you. Two of my favorite things. Yes, I think I'd like that. And I know Micah will be thrilled."

"What, pizza gets top billing? I'll have to work extra hard to change your mind this weekend when I take you out on a real date."

"That sounds like a challenge."

"Only to myself. How about if I pick you guys up in an hour? That'll give me a few minutes to make a phone call."

"To your mom?"

"Yeah. She'd kill me if she finds out I didn't talk to her the instant I knew for sure. But…I had to talk to you first."

"Call her. We'll be waiting."

He smiled, amazed at his luck. Annie was one special woman.

"And Drew?"

"Yeah."

"Thanks for letting me know first."

Drew was still smiling when he said goodbye and ended the conversation. There was a new depth, a new understanding between them. He'd always thought sex led to intimacy, not the other way around, but now he had to wonder. Maybe God knew what He was talking about after all?

ANNIE IGNORED THE FLUTTER of excitement when the doorbell rang.

"Daddy!" Micah ran to the door and jumped up and down. "Open."

Laughing, she said, "I will, be patient. I have to get the big lock."

She flipped the childproof lock at the same time Micah grasped the knob and twisted.

"Oh, no, you don't." She picked him up and made gobbling noises on his neck while she swung the door open.

Drew stood there, an eyebrow raised. He looked as happy as she felt.

"There's two of my favorite people."

"Daddy!" Micah scrambled to get down and launch himself at Drew's knees, where he wrapped him in a pint-size bear hug.

Drew snatched him up and tossed him into the air. "Hey, kid, I missed you. It's been too long."

"It's been less than twenty-four hours," Annie pointed out.

"That's what I said. It's been *way* too long." Their gazes locked, and the temperature seemed to rise along with the double meaning.

The suspense was frustrating…and exciting. By the time they finally made love, it would probably only take one touch from him and she'd be over the edge in an instant.

"Let me get Micah's jacket just in case it's chilly when we come home."

"Yeah, the weather's turned. It may even be a cool Thanksgiving."

"I'd be even happier with a cool Halloween. Micah's costume is bound to be hot otherwise." She grabbed his jacket from the coat closet and swung her purse over her shoulder. "Okay, let's go. I'm starving."

"Pizza." Micah clapped his hands.

Annie couldn't seem to stop smiling. It felt as if the hard times were behind them and only good things could happen. And it was all wrapped up with Drew.

DREW CHUCKLED AS HE listened to Micah chatter away and chew a bite of pizza at the same time, amazed that the boy had been able to talk and eat for a half hour straight. Because of his age, Micah wasn't very efficient at either task, which made for an interesting dining experience.

"Slow down, buddy, we don't want you to choke."

Annie gave the boy a stern look. "Remember, I said not to talk with your mouth full?"

But nothing could stop Micah tonight. They heard all about preschool and the children in his class, unrelated stories that came out in disjointed fragments.

Drew loved every minute of it. Just as he loved the relaxed atmosphere in the neighborhood pizza place. They seemed like a regular family catching a meal.

Annie sighed. "I don't know why I bother trying to teach him manners."

"Because you love him, and while you're relieved he's a social kid, you don't want him to be the weird one who grosses out all the other kids in the cafeteria."

"Very perceptive." She smiled and sipped her soft drink. "Tell me about your day."

"Nothing out of the ordinary. Did a couple of home appraisals today. It's a nice change of pace from all the commercial stuff I do. Most times I get to meet the homeowner and hear the stories of what they've done to make a house a home."

"Saving ideas for when you have your own?"

He grinned. "I have to admit, I've thought more about getting a house since I found out about Micah. I need a place with more space, and a backyard for him to play in."

"He'd like that."

Drew held her hand, rubbing her knuckles with his thumb, wondering how she would feel about a permanent commitment. But he didn't want to push her or their relationship that fast.

"So how was your day?" he asked.

"Good. Brett was—"

Drew's cell phone started playing reveille, signaling that it was one of his army buddies. He held up a finger to tell Annie to hold that thought while he flipped open the device, noting the familiar number.

"Hey, Steve—"

"It's Vanessa, Drew. I need your help." Her voice was strained.

"What's the matter? Are you crying?"

"It's Steve. He needs you. Come quick, we're at home."

There was a clunking sound, as if the phone had been dropped.

"Vanessa?"

There was no answer; the line was dead.

"What is it?" Annie asked.

"There's something wrong with Steve. I need to get to his house right away." He thought for a minute. "I don't want to leave you here, and it's in the opposite direction from your house."

"We'll go with you. I'll get a box for the pizza."

"No, I don't want you two there. I'm not sure what's going on." And didn't know how bad off Steve might be.

"We'll sit in the truck until you tell us everything is okay. Now you're wasting time. Go pull the truck around while I get a box."

Drew hesitated, but the panic he'd heard in Vanessa's voice… "Okay."

He kissed Annie quickly, then headed for the door.

ANNIE SAT IN THE TRUCK with the windows cracked to let in fresh air.

Glancing at the backseat, she was reassured to see Micah still sleeping. He'd exhausted himself in his excitement at the restaurant. And for that she was grateful.

Music played softly from the CD player, but she was far from relaxed. Drew had left the keys in the ignition and had told her to drive away if it sounded as if things were growing heated in the house.

She shuddered, hoping she wouldn't have to choose between getting her son to safety and helping Drew if he needed her. She liked Vanessa and Steve, and wouldn't be hiding out here in the truck if it weren't for Micah.

Drew's grim expression while he drove had told her this wasn't a minor spat or plumbing emergency. He'd even gone so far as to say he hoped they wouldn't need the police.

Annie checked the clock on the dash. It had only been fifteen minutes since they'd arrived, but it seemed like hours.

Nearly ten minutes later, Vanessa emerged from the house, her posture stiff.

Annie got out of the truck and went to her. "Is everything okay?"

Vanessa shook her head, tears spilling down her cheeks. "Drew says to drive over to the grocery store on the next block and give him half an hour, and then call him first before returning. He's got his cell out and ready to dial 911. Otherwise, I wouldn't leave."

"Tell me what's going on."

"We were arguing and…Steve just flipped out. Screaming and throwing things. He's *never* done that before. He was like someone I didn't know."

Annie touched the other woman's arm. "Did he hurt you?"

"No. But he wanted to. I could see it in his eyes… He locked himself in the master bedroom instead. I could hear him in there, breaking things, and then it got quiet… I didn't know what to do, so I called Drew."

"I'm not leaving, by the way," Annie stated.

"That's what he thought you'd say. I'm supposed to tell you to get your pretty butt out of here and keep Micah safe. I'd rather you drove, but I will if I have to. He told me the keys were in the ignition."

Drew had figured Annie wouldn't let Vanessa drive off with Micah in the truck. Just as he'd realized their son's safety would have to come first.

Annie hesitated, but knew she had no choice. "I'll drive. Get in."

Vanessa's shoulders slumped as she went to the passenger side of the truck and opened the door. She paused and stared at the house in disbelief, her eyes swollen and red.

Annie climbed in the driver's seat and started the engine. Vanessa took the passenger seat and closed the door, securing her seat belt as if by rote. "And he gave me another message. He says he loves you."

Fear gripped Annie as she reversed down the driveway. Fear for Drew's safety.

And the realization that she might never recover if something happened to him.

I love you, too, Drew.

CHAPTER TWENTY-ONE

THE MASTER BEDROOM was cool, but Drew wiped perspiration from his eyes. He smelled fear—his, Steve's. His scalp tingled like it used to when he was on patrol, indicating danger. It was a sixth sense that had never steered him wrong.

Steve leaned against the wall next to the dresser, swaying slightly, a bottle of vodka in one hand and a pistol in the other.

"Can't stay here." He gestured with the bottle.

Drew was relieved he didn't use the gun to punctuate his point. Yet.

"Why not?" he asked

"I almos' hurt her." Steve stopped swaying for a moment. Tears trickled down his face. "Be better off without me."

Drew resisted the urge to glance at the gun.

Instead, he focused on his friend. He had to help Steve get to a safe place where he could get medical care. Before he did something stupid. And permanent.

"Vanessa loves you."

"She's...scared of me."

"You're not yourself, buddy. I know you would never hurt Vanessa. She knows it, too. We just need to get you some treatment." He stepped closer.

Steve raised the pistol, stared at it as if wondering how it got in his hand. "Just can't do it, Drew. I've tried. But it's worse. The night sweats. And feeling like I'm gonna jump outta my skin. I thought it'd get better once I was home. Normal. Nothin's normal anymore."

"Man, I hate seeing you hurting like this. Did you tell anyone over there?"

"Nobody to tell. No replacement for Orion yet." He drank from the bottle. "Did' ya know? Orion's dead?"

Drew's gut twisted. He felt as if Steve had pinpointed Drew's cause for shame and was shining a spotlight on it. But he knew better. His friend was too mired in his own crap to bother pointing out someone else's.

"I was there when it happened, remember?"

"Yeah." He swayed, held the gun up for closer inspection. "I wonder if it hurts when you die?"

"I figure I don't want to find out until I'm an

old man, and then I want to go in my sleep. I want to live to see my grandchildren." He realized it with searing intensity. And he wanted Annie there next to him, growing old with him.

"Can't make babies with Nessa. Even that doesn't work anymore."

Drew winced. He felt totally unequipped for this. But there was no one else.

God, help me get this right. Steve deserves to be safe and well. And while we're at it, would You keep me safe and well, too?

"It's because of the PTSD. Once we get you the right treatment, everything will go back to normal."

"You promise?"

"I promise. Now give me the gun." He stepped closer.

"Get back." Steve raised the pistol. His hand trembled, his knuckles were white.

Get back.

Drew felt as if there was an echo in the room.

He moved back, one step, two. And held his breath.

Slowly, Steve lowered the gun.

Go to the window.

Shaking his head, Drew wondered if he was losing his mind.

Go to the window, check on Annie.

Annie. Was she still outside? Or had she followed his instructions and taken Micah and Vanessa to safety?

"I'll give you some room, buddy." He backed up, step by step, until he reached the window. Turning, he peered through the blinds, relieved to see the driveway was empty.

"Get away from the window! Sniper!"

He half turned and Steve tackled him.

Drew's breath was knocked out of him as they hit the floor. It felt as if his chest was compressed, and the pain in his ribs was agonizing.

He rolled, his lungs burning as he sucked in oxygen. "It's okay…no snipers…here."

Steve turned on his back and shook his head as if to clear it. "We're…okay?"

"Yeah…we're okay." Drew staggered to his feet and assessed the situation.

Steve lay on the floor, vodka bottle raised as if to save it. His other hand was empty.

And the gun was at Drew's feet.

He snatched it up and unloaded it, palming the cartridge into the pocket of his jeans.

Steve was passed out, mouth open, snoring lightly, the bottle still gripped in his hand.

ANNIE STARED AT THE clock on the dash for about the millionth time. She flipped open her cell phone to make sure she hadn't missed a call or received a text message.

She hadn't.

Vanessa did the same with her phone.

"Nothing. I'm calling Drew." She pushed one button and waited for the connection. After a short time, she muttered a curse and closed her phone. "He doesn't answer."

Annie was more afraid than she'd ever been. Including the time she'd been suspended over Devil's Canyon with only a battered guardrail standing between her and death. And her date thinking it was funny.

"I'm calling 911," she said.

Vanessa hesitated. Then she raised her chin. "No, I will. It's my house. Steve's my husband."

But Drew's my world.

Annie swallowed hard as she watched Vanessa punch three short digits, numbers that had the power to change her life forever. For better or worse.

Annie couldn't believe she'd managed to put herself in the kind of situation she had been determined to avoid. She loved a man who had willingly walked into a dangerous situation.

To save his friend.

He'd acted with the strength and goodness

she'd sensed in Drew the first time she'd met him. And now who he was might take him away from her forever.

"I need to report an emergency situation…." Vanessa sounded faraway as she gave her address. "Already on their way? Thank you."

Annie began to tremble.

"They received a 911 call from my house. Annie, we've got to get over there."

Annie nodded, turning the key in the ignition.

She drove by rote, feeling numb. It seemed hours later when they arrived, but couldn't have been more than a few minutes. Red and blue flashing lights illuminated the neighborhood like some sort of Fourth of July block party, complete with neighbors out in the street.

Annie screeched to a halt near a fire truck. There were two police cars and an ambulance, too.

"Fire truck!" Micah pointed.

"Yes, sweetie, a fire truck."

Vanessa flung open the door and jumped out, running toward the ambulance.

Annie wanted to follow. No, she wanted to outrun her and make sure it wasn't Drew in that ambulance. But her son kept her anchored to the truck. Whatever was happening, she was sure Micah didn't need to see it.

The paramedics wheeled out a gurney. She strained to see.

Vanessa touched the man on the gurney, grasped his hand and kissed it.

It had to be Steve. But where was Drew? Inside the house? Dead?

Annie glanced at Micah, torn. Her eyes burned. What if Drew was hurt?

She wiped tears from her face.

"Daddy!"

He was headed toward them across the lawn.

She flung open the door and dashed to meet him, flinging herself into his arms. Her heart beat wildly as she held him, reassured herself that he was real, he was alive. Stepping back, she ran her hands over his arms and chest, making sure there were no injuries.

"You're okay?"

He gave her a whisper of a smile. "Yeah, I'm okay. Better now that you're here. I want to hold my son."

"Absolutely."

They walked around to the back door. Drew opened it and pulled Micah out of his car seat. He held him tight to his chest, rocking back and forth as they watched the paramedics load Steve in the ambulance.

Annie wrapped her arm around Drew waist,

resting her cheek against his shoulder. "Is he going to be okay?"

"I wish I knew."

DREW'S ADRENALINE STARTED to wear off about the time they reached the hospital. He was grateful Annie had insisted on driving.

He kissed her. "You two take the truck home. Someone'll drive me over to pick it up tomorrow."

"I'm staying. I called Kat while you were talking to the officer, and she's coming here to pick up Micah. I'll meet you inside after they leave. Now go."

"I'm not sure I'll be decent company."

"I don't need to be entertained. I just need to be there and know you're okay. And I want to be there for Vanessa and Steve, too."

Part of him was grateful. Another part wished she'd go home and leave him to muddle through his confusing thoughts and emotions alone. Something had changed tonight and he needed time to process the ramifications.

But he was too exhausted to argue with her.

Nodding, he got out of the truck. He went around to Micah's door and leaned in to kiss his soft baby cheek. "Love ya, buddy. Be good for Auntie Kat."

Micah smiled sleepily and waved.

Drew turned and squared his shoulders, wondering if the ordeal at Steve's house might be the easy part compared to what was ahead.

He didn't know much about this kind of thing, but he suspected Steve would be admitted to the psychiatric ward.

He found Vanessa in the waiting room, pacing.

"Have you heard anything yet?" he asked her.

"No. They said something about detox, but that's for drug addicts and alcoholics." She twisted the strap of her purse. "He has drunk more since he's been back, but surely he doesn't need detox."

Putting his arm around her shoulder, Drew said, "He needs help. Let's see what the professionals say, okay? No matter what, I'm here for you two. I'll help you through whatever comes."

"Thanks, Drew. I don't know what I would have done without you. I was afraid they'd... call in a SWAT team and kill him. I knew the only one who could help him was someone who had been over there with him. Someone who could understand."

"Sir?"

Drew looked up to see the investigating officer.

"You did good tonight." He stuck out his hand and Drew shook it.

"Thank you, but I was just being a friend."

"He'll need that friendship in the coming weeks. It's good for him to know he's not alone."

"You sound like you speak from experience," Annie said as she joined them.

"My brother-in-law was messed up when he came back. But my wife's sister is a bulldog. She kept at them until she got what he needed."

The spark Drew had felt earlier seemed to grow, until he felt consumed with determination.

"It shouldn't be this way. The guys have no idea what they're in for when they get home. Steve couldn't understand why he wasn't the man he was before. Why these things were happening to him."

Officer Kilpatrick shook his head. "Well, I need to gather some information from the staff for my report. Good luck to you." He nodded and left.

Annie touched Vanessa's arm. "Why don't you sit down? I'll go get some coffee."

"Thanks. I could use it." Vanessa made herself as comfortable as she could on one of the vinyl waiting room chairs.

Annie hugged Drew tightly, then went in search of the cafeteria.

Drew sat next to Vanessa.

He stared out the window. What had seemed an impossibility the first time Beth had broached the subject, now seemed preordained. He couldn't turn his back on people like Steve. He would have to go where he was needed most...even if it meant losing Annie. He wouldn't be able to live with himself otherwise.

Drew watched as she returned with a cardboard tray holding three cups of coffee. Fatigue left faint smudges beneath her eyes. With her glasses, she looked like a student cramming for finals.

A deep, aching sense of loss enveloped him.

CHAPTER TWENTY-TWO

ANNIE SIGHED WITH relief when they pulled into her apartment complex parking lot at 5:00 a.m. It was still dark out, but she knew it would be light all too soon.

"Thank goodness Kat's going to drop off Micah at preschool. I'll call in a personal day myself and try to get some sleep."

Drew put the truck in park. "Um, thanks, Annie. You've been great about all this."

His response puzzled her. It was oddly formal for someone who had recently professed his love for her, albeit through a third party.

But they were both tired. "I'd like to think Vanessa and Steve would do the same for us if the circumstances were reversed."

"I'm sure they would. Well, I'll walk you to your door."

Again, the strange politeness sent her on red alert.

"Sure."

They walked in silence. When they arrived at her door, Drew kissed her on the cheek. "Sleep well."

"You could stay. I mean, we don't have to sleep together or anything. Well, sleep together, but not have sex. It would be nice to have someone to hold."

Drew frowned. "Annie, can I come inside for just a minute?"

"Sure." She opened the door and walked in, flicking on the light. Once inside, she turned. "Did you mean what you said, Drew? That you love me?"

"We need to talk."

"Oh, great. You tell me through a third party that you love me, scare me half to death thinking you'd been killed by your friend and then you give me the 'let's talk' bit. Don't you see anything even a little contradictory about this?"

"I'm sorry."

Annie felt as if she were about to shatter. Exhaustion combined with running the emotional gauntlet left her…fragile. Or maybe it was opening herself up, only to get the boot. Because that's sure what it felt like.

"What are you sorry about, Drew?"

"I can't be what you need me to be." He ran

his hand through his hair. She used to find this habit of his endearing. "You need someone who will make you feel safe. You said yourself you couldn't handle a guy who took risks."

Relief washed over her. She went to him and wrapped her arms around his waist. "You took a risk tonight and it was scary. I'll admit I don't want to ever go through something like that again. But we got through it. When I had to leave you there, I realized how much I love you. I didn't intend for it to happen, it just did. And you said you loved me."

He made a noise low in his throat. "I do love you, Annie. I meant that I didn't want to leave that unsaid if…something happened."

"I know."

"But I also realized something in that hospital tonight. I'm needed back in Iraq or wherever the soldiers are. I can't stand on the sidelines. Being a chaplain is something I feel I'm called to do. And if I'm going to do it, I need to go where God sends me."

Annie paced, trying to find some way she didn't have to give him up. "Are you sure you aren't just getting cold feet because you told me you loved me? You're not even that religious."

Hurt flashed in his eyes. He raised his chin. "In my own way, I have a strong faith. And with the proper training, I can give these guys the kind of counsel they need. It won't be easy, but I know it's what I have to do. I can't turn my back on that."

"But you'll turn your back on us?" It felt as if the words were torn straight from her heart.

"Annie." He touched her cheek. "We feel so right it amazes me, and I want so much for us to be a family. But I know you. I know the risks I'll be taking would destroy you."

Annie cast about for a solution that wouldn't mean she'd lose him. "How can you be sure you're not called to be a chaplain here in the States? There's a need here, too. You saw that for yourself tonight."

He leaned back, grasping her shoulders. "That's not where I'm being led. I *am* sure I'm needed in Iraq, where there are so many soldiers struggling with an enemy they can't see, can't fight. And who feel as if they're fighting alone."

Gazing up into his wonderful eyes, she blinked back tears. There was no compromise here, no easy fix.

She skimmed her fingertips over his face. "The first thing I noticed about you was the kindness in your eyes. You're loyal to the bone and care so much about people. And it's just so obscene that the things I love most about you should tear us apart."

"I know." He closed his eyes. "I wish there was another way." Opening his eyes, he said, "And I can't ask you to overcome your fear. I'd be trying to change you and I love you just the way you are. It's a catch-22 that neither of us can resolve."

"Maybe I *can* change," she whispered.

He tipped her chin up with his finger. "Can you honestly tell me you could handle being a chaplain's wife? Never knowing if I was safe? Never knowing if that knock on the door is going to come?"

Annie remembered seeing her father's broken body at the base of the mountain, remembered the way her mother had disintegrated in her grief.

Her voice was hoarse with tears as she said, "No, I can't tell you that."

Their relationship was over. She could see it in his eyes as he turned and left, the apartment door shutting behind him.

THE NEXT FEW WEEKS were the hardest of Annie's life. Drew arranged his work schedule so he could take Micah out to lunch every day and return him to preschool. It was every child's fantasy, a seemingly endless supply of Happy Meals.

She'd made the necessary arrangements with the preschool director, both relieved and disappointed that she didn't have to see Drew. It would be too difficult.

But not seeing him was agony, too. She'd come to rely on him to coparent their son. And she'd enjoyed feeling like a couple and a real family, even though they hadn't had so much as a real date. She'd felt secure with Drew.

Why did he have to spoil it?

Because he was an honorable man. And God help her, she loved him all the more for it.

Annie found she couldn't eat, couldn't sleep, couldn't seem to string together two coherent thoughts. It was hell. And yet, she couldn't help realizing that if she was in this much misery over a love affair gone bad, how incredibly bereft Steve must have felt. How terrifying it must be to think you were out of control. He'd done the right thing for the right reasons, and life as he knew it had ended. No wonder he'd started drinking heavily.

Annie made an effort to keep in touch with Vanessa to find out about his progress. There were ups and downs in his recovery, but he was determined to make it work. And now that he had the support he needed, he might just make it. His courage astounded her.

But he wouldn't have had the opportunity to recover if it hadn't been for Drew.

She was proud of Drew and his goals. She admired him more than she'd admired anyone in a long, long time. And she grieved because of the huge hole he'd left in her life. A hole she'd never known existed until he appeared on her doorstep and showed her how to love completely.

If the nights were long, weekends seemed never ending. One Saturday, she felt particularly restless. It was as if she had to go somewhere, do *something* or she was going to explode.

Annie called her mother to see if she would welcome an impromptu trip to the cabin. But her mom was uncharacteristically flustered, saying it wasn't a good weekend. Upon hearing a male chuckle in the background, Annie got the impression she'd be cramping her style.

"Do you want to go for a drive, sweetie?" she asked Micah.

"See Daddy?"

"No, we're not going to see Daddy. Just a drive."

Micah hugged her around the legs. Despite her show of good cheer, he seemed to sense her sadness. "Drive."

Annie packed some snacks and the diaper bag, and they were soon on the road.

First destination, Kat's apartment.

Annie sang along to Micah's *Veggie Tales* CD, but it only reminded her of Drew, who had shown him the wonders of the creative stories.

"Do you want to listen to something else, sweetie?" She glanced in the rearview mirror.

"No. *Veggie Tales.*"

Annie felt guilty for wishing Micah would fall asleep so she could change the music. She was a horrible mother. And a horrible person.

She wished Drew was here to tell her she was a terrific mom again.

On the way to Kat's, they passed the pizza place where Drew had taken them to dinner. They'd felt like a real family there. Until Vanessa had called.

"Daddy!"

"Where?"

Micah pointed out the window at a man in a blue truck who bore only a vague resemblance to Drew.

"No, he just looks a little like Daddy," Annie said, disappointed it wasn't him.

She was noticing a trend here. Every thought seemed to turn to Drew.

She vowed not to think about him for at least five minutes.

Until she pulled into Kat's parking lot and

saw Dillon's monstrosity of a Hummer. The guy couldn't even hold a job. How in the world did he make the payments, let alone budget for gas?

Turning the car around, she commented, "It looks like Auntie Kat is busy. Maybe we'll just drive around and see if inspiration strikes."

"Gramma?"

"Sorry sweetie, she's busy."

Annie glared at Dillon's Hummer on her way past. No doubt it had been Kat who'd paid for the slick attorney who'd managed to get Dillon's driving privileges reinstated.

She wished her friend could find a good guy instead of a lowlife like Dillon. Someone honest and loyal, funny, sexy and great with kids.

Someone like Drew.

"Humph."

It was a losing battle trying not to think about him. Compared to the Dillons of this world, he was a superhero.

"I'd rather spend an hour with Drew than decades with a loser like Dillon," she muttered under her breath.

Continuing their drive, she turned down a side street about fifteen minutes later, wondering why the neighborhood seemed so familiar. Then she saw the house with the trim plants and manicured lawn, boasting toys and bikes galore. She was struck by a sense of déjà vu. She had been to this house.

On impulse, she pulled into the driveway.

"I didn't call first," she said over her shoulder to Micah. "That's poor manners. I should turn around and leave."

Her son recognized the house. "Me play. Rover, rover."

Chuckling, Annie said, "Yes, this is the house where you played Red Rover with all the kids."

He pulled at his safety harness, eager to get out.

"Okay, we'll go to the door. But they might be on their way out or something. We may not be able to stay."

"Play rover, rover!"

Annie shut off the ignition and went around to get Micah. Her heart thudded as they walked up the drive hand in hand.

But she was given no opportunity to rethink their presence, because Micah stood on his tiptoes and stretched to press the doorbell once, twice, three times before she could stop him.

Her cheeks burned and she was tempted to turn and run.

Much to her chagrin, the door opened almost immediately. She simply could not catch a break today.

CHAPTER TWENTY-THREE

BETH GREETED THEM AS if they were family. "Annie, Micah, what a wonderful surprise. Libby was telling me just the other day she wished you would come over again and play."

Beth drew them inside, leading them straight to the kitchen where a plate of cookies caught Micah's attention.

"Cookies!"

She laughed. "We just baked them. Would you like one? If it's okay with your mom, that is?"

"It's fine. Thank you for being so gracious. I should have called first instead of barging in."

"You're not barging at all. I'm so glad you came." She removed the plastic wrap from the plate and held it out to Micah. "Would you like to pick a cookie?"

His smile just about lit up the room.

"Only one, Micah," Annie warned. She had visions of him grabbing five or six.

He carefully selected the largest cookie. "Thank you."

"You're very welcome."

Libby skipped into the room. "Hi, Micah. Let's go in the backyard and play."

Placing his hand in hers, he followed her out the door without a backward glance.

"I have the feeling he'd follow her anywhere," Annie said.

"It's mutual. She enjoys feeling like the big kid when he's around. Let me get some plates and something to drink. Would you like iced tea or soda?"

"I don't want to put you to any trouble." Annie was feeling awkward, wishing she hadn't given in to the impulse to stop by.

"It's no trouble. It's nice to have someone around to fuss over. Please have a seat at the table. All the very best conversations happen in the kitchen."

Annie took the closest wooden chair at the big harvest table, relaxing as she sat. "Iced tea would be great."

Beth returned with small plates, glasses and a pitcher of iced tea, as if expecting Annie to stay a while.

Annie's vision blurred as she blinked back tears of gratitude.

"Help yourself and don't be shy. I certainly don't need any more cookies." Beth patted her hips.

Annie bit into one, even though she had no appetite at all. "Mmm."

Laughing, Beth said, "I believe chocolate chip cookies have miraculous healing qualities. They were Orion's favorite. I always made sure to bake them when he arrived home. Well, after I properly welcomed him, of course." Her eyes twinkled.

"Um, yes. I imagine he…appreciated that."

"Oh, he did. Take my word for it. We both did. That's one of the benefits of being a military wife. The reunions almost make the separations bearable. Almost."

"I don't know how you did it."

"One day at a time, like most things."

Beth watched as Annie struggled to swallow the cookie, overwhelmed by the turmoil of her emotions. Finally, the older woman said, "I saw Drew several days ago. He seemed…sad. Do you have any idea what's going on?"

She took a deep breath and said, "I haven't seen him much the past couple of weeks." Annie distracted herself with another cookie she didn't want, while she tried to pretend she wasn't dying for news of Drew.

She failed miserably. Her mouth was full when a question popped out. "Did he tell you he's going to become a chaplain?"

Beth beamed. "Yes, he did. Isn't that wonderful? Orion would have been so pleased."

How could anyone who loved Drew think this was good news? Beth, of all people, should know better.

Maybe that's exactly what had prompted Annie to seek her out.

"We…broke up."

"I thought as much. He seemed too miserable for it to be anything but romance problems."

"I'm not like you, Beth." Annie twisted her napkin, wishing things were different. "I can't just accept his decision and pretend there's no risk involved."

"Pretending doesn't do either of you any good. You need to communicate."

"You're not listening," Annie said. "There *is* no relationship."

Beth's smile faded. "It's that serious then? I'm sorry. Drew loves that son of yours, and I could have sworn he loved you, too."

"I thought so, too. But apparently not enough."

"You think if he really loved you, he wouldn't become a chaplain?"

Annie felt a twinge of guilt. Who was she to

question his calling? Truth was, she didn't question it so much as couldn't go along for the ride.

"No, I understand that he feels called to do this, and I admire it, along with his loyalty to the soldiers. I just don't understand why he can't be a chaplain here in the United States."

"You agree it's a calling?"

Hesitating, Annie said, "Yes."

"And the calling is God's will?"

"Yes...I guess so."

Beth's smile was warm and understanding, saving Annie from feeling outmaneuvered. "Then it stands to reason that God has chosen where Drew should be sharing his gift."

"But it's not fair. This isn't the way it was supposed to be. Surely it can't be God's plan that Micah could end up without a father."

"Like my children are without a father." The softness of her voice took the sting out of her rebuke.

"Oh, Beth, I'm sorry. I'm so self-centered."

"We all are. That's part of being human. The challenge is overcoming it."

"I don't think I can. I'm not calm and giving like you are. I've accepted that I need to feel more secure than most."

"Even if it means giving up Drew? Forgive

me if I'm speaking out of turn, but I don't think you'd be here if you didn't have at least a glimmer of hope that you could stand by Drew's side forever."

Was that why she was here? Had she been drawn to the one place where she would find encouragement to be the woman Drew needed her to be?

Panic welled up. "I can't. I've got…issues. I can't stand the thought of losing someone else I love."

"We all have issues. You're just coming face-to-face with what it means to be human. We're not God, we're not in control."

Annie stood, her hands clenched. "That can't be all there is. How can I ever feel truly safe if my life is just some random whim of an all-powerful God?"

"By faith. And by knowing you have a purpose. Have you thought beyond Drew's calling to your own?"

"I'm living my purpose. I'm Micah's mother and I interpret for hearing-impaired children. It's not like I'm a serial killer."

Beth laughed. "Goodness, no. All I'm saying is that maybe your purpose is entwined with Drew's."

"No. I can't accept that."

"I could be wrong. It's something to think about, though, isn't it? All I can do is share my experience. I wouldn't have traded a minute of my life with Orion, even if it meant my life would be easier. Some things are worth the struggle, the challenge. Sometimes we're called to give more than we think we're able. But when push comes to shove, we do it anyway. That's what faith is all about."

Annie wrestled with the concept. All the things she thought she'd known no longer applied.

Rubbing her temples, she said, "I know you mean well. And I appreciate you being so gracious and making time for me. But I have a terrible headache."

"Don't you see? I get so much more from our friendship than I give. Your visit was a gift, a bright spot in my day that I hadn't expected. Someday you may appreciate those gifts yourself."

Annie felt as if the room was closing in on her. "Thanks again. I have to go." She went to the back door and called frantically for Micah. When he came, she grabbed him and practically ran for the front door.

She had to get away from Beth and all her talk of faith and callings and gifts.

Plans were what mattered.

DREW GRUNTED AS he tugged on the wrench and felt primal satisfaction as the filter finally loosened. Getting dirty beneath the chassis of his truck always soothed his mind, no matter how intense the problem.

But he knew his life would look just as bleak when he rolled the creeper out from under the truck. Yes, he'd have fresh oil. But he wouldn't have Annie.

He'd given her space, hoping she'd find the courage to take a chance on him, a chance on them. It had been almost three weeks with no word from her.

Something nudged his foot.

Maybe one of the neighborhood cats. He ignored it.

It happened again, only this time it felt like a kick.

He was barely aware of knocking over the oil collection pan as he rolled out from under the truck, preparing to read someone the riot act. He was ready for an argument. He might someday be a chaplain if he made it through boot camp and religious training. But he wasn't a saint.

Shielding his eyes, he glared up at a shadowy form backlit by the noonday sun. "What the—"

"Is that any way to greet the mother of your child?"

He stood, almost afraid to believe it. "Annie?"

She tilted her head. "You have other children?"

"No. Not that I know of."

"Spoken like a true man. Always leave yourself an out."

"Hey, what gives?" He was the good guy here.

"It's more like who gave up?"

"You did."

"No, I was terrified. I needed to work through my fear, to find enough faith to accept my calling despite being scared to death. *You* gave up."

"Your calling?"

"You think *you're* the only one with a calling?"

"Um, no, but—"

Her shoulders slumped. "You gave up on me, Drew. The guy who loved me just as I was gave up on me."

The pain and loss in her eyes made him want to grab her and never let her go. But there was too much at stake.

"Annie, I'm trying to be realistic. You don't do risk. You've been very up-front about that."

"If you're too realistic, you miss out on faith. I have a calling, Drew. I'm convinced I have many purposes, and one of them is to be your wife, wherever that leads us. I will have faith that we'll get through the bad times and treasure every moment of the good times."

"Wow." That was all he could think of to say. This complex, sometimes contradictory woman wanted to share her life with him. "I love you, Annie. You and Micah are my life."

"Good. Then I know you'll do everything possible to protect what we have together. And I'll have faith that you'll stay safe and always come home to me. Because I love you more than I ever imagined possible." Her voice trailed off. That's when he noticed the tears running down her face.

Drew pulled her close, ignoring the oil pooling around their feet.

"Always, Annie. Always."

EPILOGUE

ANNIE TEETERED ACROSS the parking lot on her ridiculously high stilettos. Take-me-now shoes, or so she hoped.

Annie smiled. *She* certainly wanted to be taken—over and over again. Both grandmas were watching the kids for the entire weekend and that meant plenty of hot, sweaty, ill-advised sex for her. Ending a six-month stint of celibacy while Drew had traveled to various outposts in the Middle East. And he'd specifically requested her Goth hooker outfit for this anniversary date.

Fighting the urge to readjust the new red thong she had bought for this special occasion, Annie eyed the expanse of asphalt looming between her and the side entrance to the lounge. The mid-May Arizona heat and synthetic fabric made her perspire in places she didn't want to think about. Déjà vu. But it would all be worth-while when she saw the look of admiration on her husband's face. And got to the best part of their welcome-home tradition.

Squaring her shoulders, she stumbled onward. She could do this. She'd endured worse than the Lycra miniskirt from hell. She'd endured childbirth, not once, but twice—the second with twins. She'd gotten through Micah falling out of a tree and breaking his arm while Drew was overseas. And cared for two children under the age of three when she'd gone for weeks at a stretch without hearing from him. Thank goodness for Beth and the other military wives, who were like a second family.

Finally, Annie stepped inside the dimly lit lounge. After the harsh angle of the afternoon sun, she was effectively blinded, only able to discern vague shapes and shadows.

She detected movement as a human form separated itself from the bar and approached.

Blinking, Annie threw herself at the man. Even without her glasses, she would know him anywhere. He wrapped his strong arms around her and held her tight, murmuring words of love in her hair. Then he kissed her, showing how much he'd missed her.

Annie lost herself in his embrace, holding him tight, refusing to let go. It didn't matter that they were in a public place and a murmur of approval spread around them.

Finally, they drew apart, still touching hands as if to make sure this was real, even if it was supposed to be a fantasy. Sometimes real life was even better than anything Annie could have imagined.

Drew cleared his throat, apparently getting into character. "Um, Grace?"

Annie remembered who she was for the evening. "Uh, yes, that's me. Grace. You're Drew?"

"Yes."

She extended her hand at the same time he leaned in for a hug. He stopped and extended his hand at the same time she retracted hers and leaned stiffly from the waist.

Somehow, they managed to approximate an awkward hug.

Annie sighed. The role-playing was an anniversary tradition, but this year she would have preferred to take him to a dark, secluded hotel room right away and make mad, passionate love to him and never stop.

"I'm glad you took pity on me and came out on such short notice," he said.

Annie forced herself to get back into the script. The sooner they dispensed with this lovely, yet frustratingly public foreplay, the sooner they could get naked together.

"Um, no problem. Kat said you're shipping out in a couple of days?"

"Yeah." He touched her elbow. "How about that booth over there?"

Annie sighed in relief as she slid onto the bench. Her feet were killing her.

Drew followed, sitting near enough for their thighs to touch.

She didn't know if she could handle being so close to him without wanting to touch every inch of his body, making sure he'd come home as unscathed as he claimed.

His warm, brown eyes reflected every bit of the need she felt. He fairly oozed testosterone—from the top of his nearly shaved head, past his tanned, hard biceps, to his sculpted abs.

Sneaking one last, longing glance down his fine form, Annie suppressed a need so intense it nearly took her breath away.

Drew waited, an eyebrow raised. Oh, yeah, the script.

She licked her lips in what she hoped was an inviting way. "So, you're in the army?"

"Reserves. Got called up for another tour of active duty."

"I'm sorry. That's got to be rough."

"It's hard on my mom. She worries."

"Yes, mothers have a way of doing that. So do wives."

The waitress placed cocktail napkins on the table and glanced at Annie. "What can I get you?"

"Long Island Iced Tea." She glanced at her date and said, "They make me really...hot."

Drew ordered a beer and held up a twenty dollar bill. "This is your tip if you get those drinks here in less than five minutes."

The waitress rushed off, ignoring a customer who tried to get her attention. She seemed intent on earning that twenty.

Annie glanced around the lounge, grateful it never seemed to change from year to year. This was their special place.

"Can you tell me about where you're going?" she asked.

He shook his head. "It's sensitive."

"That means dangerous?"

He hesitated.

Beneath the table, she trailed her fingers up his thigh. She could hardly wait to get him alone and explore every inch of his body, getting reacquainted.

Drew shrugged. "I'll be in a...hot spot."

"You certainly will," she purred.

"Hey, I don't remember you saying that."

"So sue me." She moved her hand a little higher.

Groaning, he shifted in his seat, leaning in to nibble her earlobe.

This was so not in the script. And she totally approved.

He murmured her name, his mouth deliciously close to her ear, a sound so familiar, so welcome, she wanted to cry.

"Let's get out of here."

"I thought you'd never ask."

Drew threw another twenty on the table; they slid out of the booth and left as quickly as her stilettos would allow.

Annie wanted to savor every moment of having her husband to herself for the next forty-eight hours. Because once they got home, it would be kids and dogs and in-laws—all the safe chaos they'd ever wanted.

* * * * *

*Celebrate Harlequin's 60th anniversary with
Harlequin® Superromance®
and the DIAMOND LEGACY miniseries!*

*Follow the stories of four cousins as they
come to terms with the complications of love
and what it means to be a family.
Discover with them the
sixty-year-old secret that rocks not one but
two families in...
A DAUGHTER'S TRUST
by Tara Taylor Quinn.*

*Available in September 2009 from
Harlequin® Superromance®*

RICK'S APPOINTMENT with his attorney early Wednesday morning went only moderately better than his meeting with social services the day before. The prognosis wasn't great—but at least his attorney was going to file a motion for DNA testing. Just so Rick could petition to see the child…his sister's baby. The sister he didn't know he had until it was too late.

The rest of what his attorney said had been downhill from there.

Cell phone in hand before he'd even reached his Nitro, Rick punched in the speed dial number he'd programmed the day before.

Maybe foster parent Sue Bookman hadn't received his message. Or had lost his number. Maybe she didn't want to talk to him. At this point he didn't much care what she wanted.

"Hello?" She answered before the first ring was complete. And sounded breathless.

Young and breathless.

"Ms. Bookman?"

"Yes. This is Rick Kraynick, right?"

"Yes, ma'am."

"I recognized your number on caller ID," she said, her voice uneven, as though she was still engaged in whatever physical activity had her so breathless to begin with. "I'm sorry I didn't get back to you. I've been a little…distracted."

The words came in more disjointed spurts. Was she jogging?

"No problem," he said, when, in fact, he'd spent the better part of the night before watching his phone. And fretting. "Did I get you at a bad time?"

"No worse than usual," she said, adding, "Better than some. So, how can I help?"

God, if only this could be so easy. He'd ask. She'd help. And life could go well. At least for one little person in his family.

It would be a first.

"Mr. Kraynick?"

"Yes. Sorry. I was… Are you sure there isn't a better time to call?"

"I'm bouncing a baby, Mr. Kraynick. It's what I do."

"Is it Carrie?" he asked quickly, his pulse racing.

"How do you know Carrie?" She sounded defensive, which wouldn't do him any good.

"I'm her uncle," he explained, "her mother's—Christy's—older brother, and I know you have her."

"I can neither confirm nor deny your allegations, Mr. Kraynick. Please call social services." She rattled off the number.

"Wait!" he said, unable to hide his urgency. "Please," he said more calmly. "Just hear me out."

"How did you find me?"

"A friend of Christy's."

"I'm sorry I can't help you, Mr. Kraynick," she said softly. "This conversation is over."

"I grew up in foster care," he said, as though that gave him some special privilege. Some insider's edge.

"Then you know you shouldn't be calling me at all."

"Yes… But Carrie is my niece," he said. "I need to see her. To know that she's okay."

"You'll have to go through social services to arrange that."

"I'm sure you know it's not as easy as it sounds. I'm a single man with no real ties and I've no intention of petitioning for custody. They aren't real eager to give me the time of day. I never even knew Carrie's mother. For all intents and purposes, our mother didn't raise either one of us. All I have going for me is half a set of genes. My lawyer's on it, but it could be weeks—months—before this is sorted out. Carrie could be adopted by then. Which would be fine, great for her, but then I'd have lost my chance. I don't want to take her. I won't hurt her. I just have to see her."

"I'm sorry, Mr. Kraynick, but..."

* * * * *

Find out if Rick Kraynick will ever have a chance to meet his niece.
Look for A DAUGHTER'S TRUST by Tara Taylor Quinn, available in September 2009.

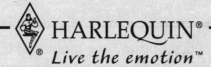

HARLEQUIN® *Romance*®

The rush of falling in love

Cosmopolitan
international settings

Believable, feel-good stories
about today's women

The compelling thrill
of romantic excitement

It could happen to you!

EXPERIENCE HARLEQUIN ROMANCE!

Available wherever Harlequin books are sold.

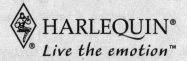 HARLEQUIN®
Live the emotion™

www.eHarlequin.com

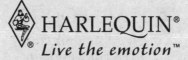

HARLEQUIN®
INTRIGUE®

BREATHTAKING ROMANTIC SUSPENSE

Shared dangers and passions lead to electrifying
romance and heart-stopping suspense!

Every month, you'll meet six new heroes
who are guaranteed to make your spine tingle
and your pulse pound. With them you'll enter
into the exciting world of Harlequin Intrigue—
where your life is on the line
and so is your heart!

THAT'S INTRIGUE—
ROMANTIC SUSPENSE
AT ITS BEST!

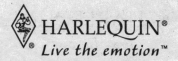

HARLEQUIN®
Live the emotion™

 Harlequin® Historical
Historical Romantic Adventure!

Imagine a time of chivalrous knights and unconventional ladies, roquish rakes and impetuous heiresses, rugged cowboys and spirited frontierswomen— these rich and vivid tales will capture your imagination!

Harlequin Historical...
they're too good to miss!

HHDIR06

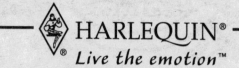